THE JAGUAR

RIVERFORD SHIFTERS BOOK TWO

CRISTINA RAYNE

Fantastical Press

Copyright © 2015 Cristina Rayne
Published by Fantastical Press
All Rights Reserved

www.CristinaRayneAuthor.com

ISBN-10: 0692530916
ISBN-13: 978-0692530917

*Dedicated to all lovers of shifter romances and
their endless enthusiasm for the next story*

ALSO BY CRISTINA RAYNE

Elven King
Claimed by the Elven King
Claimed by the Elven Brothers: Decision (Novella #1)
Claimed by the Elven Brothers: Fate (Novella #2)
Shadows Beneath the Falling Snow (A Prequel Short Story)

Riverford Shifters
Tempted by the Jaguar
Accepting the Jaguar
Rescued? by the Wolf Novella
Tempted by the Tiger *coming soon

Erotic Tales from the Vampire Underground
Blood Escort: A Short Story

Incarnations of Myth
Seeking the Oni Novella *coming soon

WRITING AS C.G. GARCIA

Fractured Multiverse
The Supreme Moment
Black Crimson (Blood Fire Chronicles Book 1) *coming soon

Old Souls Trilogy
Old Souls
The Ties That Bind the Soul
The Name Within His Soul *coming soon

The Golden Mage Trilogy
The Kingdom of Eternal Sorrow
The Man Within the Temple
The Last Stone Cast

CHAPTER ONE

*I*t was only there for a second, but Kylie saw it in his eyes—the initial shock, but more importantly, the fury and something that could very well be hate.

Hunter had given her his answer, and she only had herself to blame for the gut-wrenching pain she instantly felt. It was her fault for letting him get close enough to her heart that she could feel the knife of his rejection jab straight through with a savage twist.

However, Kylie didn't so much as blink as she continued to stare him down, refusing to show any kind of reaction even though she ached to see the various streams of blood oozing down his body from several gashes in his shoulders and chest. She knew the reputation of Polyshifters within the shifter clans—or more accurately, that the clans other than the lions

1

viewed her kind as utterly dangerous. Rightfully so.

There was a very good chance that Hunter would decide to attack her—last night's affection be damned—rather than allow her to explain, and no matter how much it would crush her soul, Kylie wasn't about to let him drag her back to the Elders without a fight. All those years living in fear of discovery—to just roll over and accept her fate now would be the ultimate insult to everything Paul and her adoptive mother, Laura, had sacrificed.

Yet, when Hunter stiffly turned his back to her without a word and strode over to the naked man slowly bleeding to death on the ground, she was completely taken aback. Of all the reactions she had expected, that Hunter would show her, a Polyshifter, his back wasn't one of them. What the hell was he *thinking*?

She opened her mouth, the first words of her confusion on the tip of her tongue before she closed it again without uttering a sound. Every instinct within her screamed for her to turn on her heel and flee while Hunter's attention was elsewhere.

Two people had seen her shift into a lioness and both had the power to destroy her. She needed to get out of the city now before either of them had time to really think about the implications of what had just happened. Although only Hunter knew for certain that she was a Polyshifter, it was only a matter of time before their lioness attacker figured it out, too.

Still…that Hunter hadn't attacked her, hadn't demanded answers, gave her a small, though likely foolish, hope that he might be open to an explanation, maybe even needed one.

Kylie stood frozen in indecision for a couple of more beats before the jacket she had borrowed from Hunter caught her eye, lying a few feet to her left in a discarded heap next to the ruined pieces of the rest of her clothes. She quietly, cautiously, moved to retrieve it without taking her eyes from that rigid and slightly bleeding back as Hunter knelt on the ground and reached for the wolf shifter's neck. Whatever she decided, she definitely didn't want to be naked for it.

As she slipped the jacket on, momentarily having a *déjà vu* of the first time she had been naked in front of Hunter when the hem just barely covered all her naughty bits, Hunter began applying pressure to the worst of the wolf shifter's back wounds. Kylie felt a huge surge of relief at that action. He wouldn't have bothered if the wolf wasn't still alive.

Kylie took a step towards them, on edge and unsure about what his sudden silence meant, but intent on helping him with the still-bleeding man. Hunter instantly jerked his head around and snarled in warning. She froze.

"*Don't* come any closer!" he warned, his rough tone making her want to crouch defensively and hiss back at him in equal warning.

She fisted her hands until she could feel her nails cutting into her palms. No—she needed to react as a human for this. Snarling at him could very likely set his jaguar off dangerously.

"Let me help you help him, Hunter," Kylie pleaded. Now that the cat was out of the bag, so to speak, about her Polyshifter heritage, she didn't have to worry about getting the wolf's blood on her skin and possibly triggering another change in her dominant shifter soul. "You can't stop all his bleeding alone."

She moved to take another step, and he growled, the sound low and menacing.

"*Don't,*" Hunter repeated. "I can't—" His voice cut off, and that same look of betrayal and hurt flashed in his eyes.

...I can't trust you, Kylie internally finished for him in rising despair. It was nothing more than she deserved. After all, she, herself, hadn't trusted *him* enough to confide the truth, even after everything he had done for her over the past couple of days.

"Hunter—"

"*Go.* Leave Riverford before the clans come for you," Hunter interjected in a tight voice, his eyes now double pools of barely contained pain. "Go now before I change my mind and haul you in before the Elders, myself."

Her composure in danger of cracking, Kylie clenched her jaw against the sob that wanted to claw itself out of her throat. Her whole body tightened as though getting ready to spring away, but she fought against the instinct. No—there was one last thing she had to say or she would regret it forever.

She took a deep, shaky breath. "I was afraid to tell you that I was a Deadend from a Polyshifter family," she confessed softly. It was probably too little too late, but she just couldn't leave without saying it. "I'm sorry."

Kylie then turned sharply on her heel to dart away before Hunter could see her face crumble. She could feel a yowl of emotion wanting to burst forth from her throat, but she gritted her teeth and viciously denied herself that release. The last thing she wanted was for Hunter to hear her pain.

Her head down and barely conscious of her surroundings, Kylie just kept on running through the trees, away from Hunter, away from the hope of a happy future that had been shattered by her own carelessness.

Kylie had only known him for a couple of days. They had only connected intimately for less than a few hours, and yet that final rejection hurt just as much as learning that her parents had seemingly disappeared off the face of the earth.

When her bare feet abruptly stepped onto cold asphalt, she realized that not only was she no longer surrounded by trees, but that she was back in the parking lot of Hunter's apartment building. She skidded to a halt, her chest heaving with more than fatigue, and leaned up against the passenger door of a charcoal-colored truck.

It was then that the floodgates finally broke and the tears that had been gathering in her eyes began to roll down her wind-chilled cheeks in scalding streams. For a long, agonizing moment, Kylie just stood there hugging herself tightly, half-dressed and crying her silent tears, unable to move her thoughts past the waves of hurt that inundated her entire being.

Only when she heard a car door slam in the distance, did her awareness crawl out of the black hole of despair it had fallen into enough to realize it was worse than stupid to be standing so exposed. She sucked in a harsh, shuddering breath, hastily wiped at the tears still leaking from her eyes, and straightened. She had to move *now*.

Her car was still at her old apartment building, so as much as it pained her to do it, she had to call Paul and confess everything. The endgame decision they both had always feared was finally being forced on them.

Luckily, she had shoved her cell phone inside her jacket pocket rather than her jeans this morning. She cringed to think of what kind of fuss she would've stirred up if she had been forced to find a phone dressed in only a blood-spattered jacket, especially when shifting was now out of the question. Damned if she would *ever* shift into a lioness again if she could help it. That was as good as painting a bright, orange target on her body.

Feeling as though every eye in the city was on her, Kylie nervously glanced around the parking lot as she waited for Paul to answer his phone. She began to cautiously move back towards the tree-line at her back. She couldn't risk going into the apartment complex and possibly being cornered. Besides, Hunter's apartment was locked, and she had no way to get a key.

Her chest tightened painfully at the thought of her mother's bracelet still hidden in Hunter's guestroom closet. It was now likely lost to her forever. Nothing to be done now but to accept that fact and move on.

The sky had lightened to a dark gray, the clouds highlighted with pinks and oranges along the horizon. It was probably around seven in the morning. Even though Paul didn't have work today, she hoped he was already up. At this point, every second would count, no matter what path they ultimately chose to take.

Kylie wasn't sure what Hunter would decide to do once the people he had called from his clan arrived to help him with the injured wolf shifter. It was obvious that he was conflicted enough about the inadvertent revelation of her secret to send her away rather than offer her up to the Elders as the spy for the lion clans he had every right to fear she was.

Would he immediately run off to find her? Would he rat her out or keep her Polyshifter heritage to himself?

If she disappeared, how could he explain it to his clan? How much trouble was she about to cause him, someone who had shown her nothing but kindness, patience, and affection?

"Kylie? Are you all right?" Paul's urgent voice suddenly said loudly into her ear, making her jump.

"Paul!" she said anxiously into the phone. "Thank God you picked up! There's no time to explain, but I need you to come get me at my new apartment building as soon as possible. I just screwed up badly, and I have to get out of Riverford *now!*"

CHAPTER TWO

The moment Kylie saw Paul's car turn into the complex parking lot, she moved away from the truck she had been crouching behind and sprinted towards it. He hadn't even come to a complete stop before she was pulling on the passenger-side door handle.

At his raised eyebrow after giving her the once-over, Kylie hastily explained as she closed the door, "I had to shift in a hurry. This jacket was the only thing that wasn't shredded."

"I have our emergency bags in the trunk," Paul said. "Karen's waiting for us at her home. You can change there."

Kylie knew that her face still bore the obvious signs of her earlier crying, and she was relieved that he

9

had chosen not to ask her about it. At least not yet.

"She's already got some of her cougar friends watching the roads out of the city," he continued. "She offered to drive us to DFW. We'll buy tickets to somewhere far—Australia or South Korea—to muddy our trail. Then she'll rent us a car, and we can figure out where to go from there—"

"Wait a minute! Slow down!" Kylie interjected. "You haven't even heard what happened, and you're already ready to throw your life, your career in Riverford away! I'm the only one who has to leave!"

"Kylie—we talked about this," Paul said sternly. "There's no way I'm sending you out there to face the danger alone. You're a million times more important to me than any job."

"But I screwed it all up, Paul! *Everything*," Kylie moaned, lowering her face into her hands. "You shouldn't have to pay for my stupidity!"

"Tell me what happened," he said calmly as he drove out of the parking lot.

"Hunter knows I'm a Polyshifter."

Paul looked at her sharply and cursed. "Put your seatbelt on, Kylie. I'll get you out of here. I don't care if I have to run down an army of shifters, but I swear on my life, on the hopes of your parents, that I'll keep you from falling into their hands. *Any* of them."

His words made her sink down farther in her seat

in shame. "That's not the worst of it. I ended up shift-ing into—into a *lioness*."

The car abruptly swerved, causing Paul to curse a second time. "How in the blazes did *that* happen? Did you touch the wrong charm?"

She shook her head. "Hunter and I were walking in the forest behind the apartment complex when we ran across a severely injured wolf shifter. He'd been shredded to an inch of his life. Hunter called his clan for help, and while we were trying to stop the worst of his bleeding, we were attacked by a lioness. Hunter and the lioness fought. He told me to run. I should've run, but I just couldn't leave them. It was obvious the lioness was after the wolf, that she was probably the one that had injured him. Then Hunter was suddenly down and not getting up, and I had to do *something*. I shifted and...I hadn't noticed that I had gotten her blood on me, so..."

"Did the lioness see you as a jaguar at all?" Paul demanded.

"No. She was so shocked when I shifted to face her that she shifted back into her human form in order to berate me. She said that Hunter's scent was so strong on me that she had assumed I was a jaguar. Af-ter calling me a traitor and disgusting, she ran off into the forest. Even if she doesn't put two and two to-gether about me possibly being a Polyshifter, at the very least, the lions'll be after me for 'siding with the jaguar scum,' as she put it."

"I take it Hunter didn't react very well to learning your secret, either?" Paul said flatly.

"No," Kylie agreed in a small voice, her chest tightening with remembered pain.

It's your own damned fault, so get over it.

"And yet you were able to get away from him to call me…" He glanced at her sideways. "Perhaps you two were a little closer than you led me to believe."

Kylie's shoulders slumped at the implied admonishment. "Last night, we…" She trailed off and shrugged uncomfortably, unable to say it out loud. "Yeah, he let me go because he's confused, but we've only known each other for a couple of days. He told me to get out of Riverford, but he may decide he made a mistake and come after me himself. After all, he knows my scent better than anyone."

She smiled bitterly. "Shifting into a lioness, of all things, probably wasn't the best way of telling him about my true heritage. I thought maybe this time— never mind. It doesn't matter any more."

"You really liked him, didn't you?" Paul said, his expression suddenly infinitely sad.

"It doesn't matter," she repeated. Maybe if she said it enough, she could one day convince her heart that it was true.

"Kylie…"

She shook her head sharply. "I should've known better. I was momentarily seduced by the thought of finally belonging somewhere, that we both might finally be able to put down permanent roots." *I was seduced by a pair of kind, hazel eyes and a sexy smile.*

"You were prepared to be a jaguar for the rest of your life," Paul ventured, sounding strangely hesitant.

He was the type to offer his opinions freely, no matter how hard they were to hear. It was one of the things she appreciated best about her adoptive father. Hearing the uncertainty in his voice raised all sorts of red flags in her mind.

However, not even that small uncertainty in Paul's voice could distract her from the power of his words. Kylie clenched her jaw against the sob that very blatant truth nearly wrenched from deep within her. She didn't want to make things worse by crying. She didn't want to remind him to ask about the tears that had already fallen.

"Stupid, I know," she said roughly after a long moment of heavy silence.

"Don't be so hard on yourself, sweetie," he said firmly. "If anyone should be censured here, it's me for encouraging you to integrate into the jaguar clan. What I should have done was get you out of the city the first moment Hunter's back was turned. No amount of information is worth your life."

Kylie said nothing, her eyes fixed onto the trembling hands fisted so tightly in her lap that they had turned white. Only this morning she had awoken within the arms of a man she had really started to fall for, thinking that for once in her life, things may have started looking up.

She should have known better.

Her eyes fell on a bottle of water sitting in the cup holder closest to Paul. Suddenly, it was clear what she had to do.

"Paul, did you drink from this?" Kylie asked, picking up the bottle and waving it in front of his face briefly.

"Good idea," he said, nodding in approval. "Anyone looking for you will be searching for the scent of a jaguar or lioness. A human's scent is probably just background noise, so to speak, to the shifters, and where we're going, there'll be a lot of it."

Kylie unscrewed the cap. "Exactly. That's why, once I've completely repressed the shifter part of me, I don't plan on shifting ever again if I can help it."

Then before her adoptive father could reply, she rubbed her fingers vigorously over the open mouth of the bottle until the scent of Paul's anxiety and humanity, as well as Hunter's enticing scent that had been emanating from the jacket she wore, faded into the normal scents of the inside of a car that any human would smell. She rubbed her nose in a bit of relief, finding some comfort in the familiarity of a limited sense of smell, even if the ghost of Hunter's scent still lingered in her mind as a painful, yet fitting punishment for her moment of weakness.

"I suck at being a shifter. First it was the jaguar heat, then this." Kylie laughed humorlessly. "I couldn't even stay out of trouble for longer than a few hours at a time. It's probably best that I go back to being a human permanently."

Paul frowned, his disapproval practically radiating off him. "You have the rest of your life to make that decision."

"I doubt it," Kylie replied with a weary sigh. "Life seems to enjoy taking all our choices away—or forcing them."

Without taking his eyes off the road, Paul placed his hand onto Kylie's shoulder and gave it a comforting squeeze. "I'll see to it. I promise."

His words only made Kylie want to cry again, not for herself, but for him and the heavy burden her existence placed on his shoulders.

CHAPTER THREE

*H*unter's mind raced a million miles-a-minute as he watched two men from his clan hoist up the stretcher the injured red wolf had been placed onto earlier, tubes of blood and saline already feeding into two IVs that had been inserted into the underside of both pale forearms. The medical team that had been sent had managed to stabilize him enough to move him, and Needles had been optimistic about his chances. Hunter had never been so glad to see the overzealous doctor in his life, thankful that Gaither had called for him particularly.

Finally, a huge clue regarding his missing brother had fallen into his clutches. *He might be alive.* His chest ached painfully at the thought. After a year of fearing the worst, to have that fear so unexpectedly given even a tiny hope of being lain to rest was jarring.

He should have been beside himself with joy, with relief. He should have been at the very least calling Maxim to tell him to follow them to the hospital. His best friend had just as much riding on the information the wolf shifter could provide them once he had regained consciousness as Hunter did.

He bared his teeth. So why was his jaguar roaring for him to chase after Kylie *right now*? To do so would probably be the stupidest thing he had ever done in his life, including his inordinately stupid decision to sleep with her. He damn well knew that.

Yet, as he stood watching his clan brothers and sisters prepare to move the injured stranger out of the forest, he was having a tough time keeping himself from shifting. Even now, he could feel small, rebellious spasms across the muscles of his body as he held himself rigid.

A Polyshifter...

She could have lied. She could have continued to feign ignorance as she had when he had told her about Deadends and Returners. Instead, she had looked him straight in the eye and admitted it, standing there looking so strong and challenging even though she had been utterly naked in more ways than one.

Kylie had to have known that her admission could have very well ended with his teeth at her throat, so why? Hunter scowled. Nothing about the whole mess made any sense!

Why in the hell had she revealed her true nature by shifting into a *lioness* in the first place? Was it just a colossal fuck-up on her part? Caught out, did Kylie hope that the truth would somehow salvage things, that it would muddy things enough for him to drop his guard in regards to her again?

Hunter felt a growl forming deep within his chest. Was that whole string of events—from finding Kylie attacking that piece of human scum in the forest to finding the half-dead wolf to her shifting into something other than a jaguar—just part of some grand plan of infiltration by the lions?

Or did she hide the truth because she was scared that I would react badly, that we would all react badly to such a dangerous secret? Was she actually hiding from everybody...*including the humans who adopted her?*

"Why the hell didn't you call me, you asshole?" a familiar voice abruptly growled behind him, causing Hunter to jump and hiss in startlement as he whirled around.

"Maxim! What the hell are you doing here?" Hunter demanded.

Maxim looked at him incredulously. "You're seriously asking me that? Imagine my surprise when Lana called me half an hour ago to report a bunch of jaguars—*Needles* among them—scrambling out of Riverford Regional towards an ambulance and a certain *someone's* name and the words 'bleeding heavily' being mentioned among their urgent chatter…"

Hunter grabbed his upper arms. "Did you tell anyone else about this?"

Maxim snorted. "Of course not. I jumped in my car and probably broke every traffic law trying to get here. When I pounded on your door and no one answered, I followed my nose to you here." His eyes darted towards the retreating group. "Now that I know you aren't the one bleeding out in that stretcher, mind telling me what the hell happened here? And where's Kylie?"

At the mention of her name, a mixture of anger and pain surged through him, but he ruthlessly stamped it down. Now was not the time to deal with that messed up shit.

"Not here," Hunter said, giving his friend a minute shake and gesturing towards the others with his eyes. "They're taking him to my clan's private clinic. If you'll drive, I'll tell you on the way."

His eyes narrowing, Maxim merely nodded and followed Hunter out of the forest.

As soon as they had climbed into Maxim's black Mercedes, Maxim raised an eyebrow pointedly before

Hunter could even settle into the leather seat.

Hunter sighed, suddenly feeling more tired and lost than he had in a long time.

"She's a Polyshifter, Maxim."

"*Kylie?*" Maxim asked in disbelief. "You have got to be shitting me!"

Hunter didn't think he had ever seen his friend so stunned.

He sighed and closed his eyes. "You and maybe the lioness who attacked us are the only ones who know right now."

"Lioness?" Maxim echoed in alarm. "I think you need to start at the beginning."

The ambulance started to drive away, and Maxim diverted his attention for a moment to pull in behind it in order to follow.

"Kylie and I spent last night together," Hunter admitted after a long pause. "After Jennifer left, we got to talking, and well, I suppose I've done dumber things—though at the moment I'm having a hard time thinking of any."

"I doubt that very much, my friend," Maxim remarked dryly. "So you slept together. Given where I just found you, I take it you followed my suggestion and took her on your early morning patrol of your territory."

Hunter chuckled humorlessly. "We never even

got that far. We'd barely been walking for a few minutes when we both caught a whiff of blood in the air, and the wolf you just saw my clansmen spirit away dragged himself into view. How he ended up in my part of the forest looking like roadkill is anyone's guess, but believe it or not, that's not even the question I'm itching to ask him the moment he wakes up."

He turned in his seat to completely face Maxim. "Before he passed out, that wolf said my brother had sent him to find me."

The car swerved for a couple of seconds as Maxim looked at him sharply. "What the fuck?"

Hunter ran his hand through his hair in agitation. "My thoughts exactly. Here was the first real lead I've had about my brother in over a year and the man was on the verge of bleeding out right at my feet! I called for help, then Kylie and I tried to stop the bleeding as best we could. However, it wasn't long before we were attacked by a lioness. The damned bitch came out of nowhere.

"The way she moved—she had to be one of their assassins. I literally came within an inch of having my throat ripped out. I managed to kick her off me before I shifted, but I was nowhere near her fighting level. I got knocked senseless for a few moments, and that's when it happened."

He bared his teeth in renewed anger. "I told Kylie

to run, but she didn't. Instead, she shifted—into a *lioness*."

"Did she attack you?" Maxim asked quietly.

Hunter yanked on his hair viciously. "I wish she had. Then I wouldn't be so—"

He cut himself off before his tongue could betray any more of his turmoil. Damn it! They were almost at the clinic. The last thing he needed right now was to have his head messed up with thoughts of Kylie.

"While I was semi out of it, she faced off against the assassin," he continued curtly. "The lioness shifted back into a short-haired, blonde woman, spat some vitriol at Kylie, and then ran off."

"I see."

Hunter couldn't read his friend's expression. "And…?" he prodded.

"Where is she now?" Maxim asked, ignoring his question.

He looked away. "I don't know."

"You must be joking…"

"She stood right there in front of me and admitted she was a Polyshifter without so much as batting a fucking eye. My head was already spinning from both headbutting that lioness's thick skull harder than I should have and a dying wolf shifter mentioning my brother out of the blue. I didn't know what the hell to think. Plus, my clansmen were probably only a few minutes from arriving, and there was no mistaking the stench of lion coming off her."

"Fuck…you let her *go*, didn't you!" Maxim exclaimed, shaking his head.

"I did," Hunter replied hotly, his eyes daring the other man to give him shit about it.

Which of course he did.

"Damn it, Hunter!" Maxim growled. "I can't believe you let the best chance we've had *ever* to maybe find out something about a real Polyshifter just waltz on out from under your nose! If she's hidden herself so well from everyone until now, I wouldn't doubt she could do it again, and better, now that she knows for sure her cover's blown! She could be well on her way to the border by now!"

"No matter what she may have been able to tell us, there's no way we would have been able to trust it. You *know* that we can't trust *any* Polyshifter." Hunter paused and then continued with a grimace, "…and because of what happened between us, I can't trust *myself* to be objective. Right now I'm more dangerous to the Riverford clans than she is."

"You fell for her that hard?" Unlike before, there wasn't even a hint of judgment in his voice, which made Hunter feel worse.

"She deceived me. She deceived us all," Hunter said, unable to keep the hurt from his tone.

"Yes," Maxim agreed matter-of-factly. "However, I wonder about the reason. I understand why you didn't want to hand her over to the Elders, but you should have at the very least brought her to *me* to question. If she is truly an innocent in all of this—"

"—then I might very well have sent her straight into the lion's den."

That ominous sentence hung thickly in the air as they pulled into the parking lot of a group of generic-looking office buildings that were co-owned by all the jaguar Elders. Maxim followed the ambulance to the back of one of the central buildings where a group of people in scrubs were already waiting to receive them.

"I fucked up big time, didn't I?" Hunter said grimly as Maxim slid the car into an empty parking slot.

"Go on inside," Maxim said, pulling his phone from a pocket inside his sport coat. "You need to make sure you're there the moment that wolf opens his eyes. Let me worry about Kylie for now. One way or another, I'll make sure we learn the truth."

Hunter hesitated for a few more seconds before giving himself a mental kick in the ass. What the hell was he doing angsting about his love life of all things? Maxim, himself, was a reminder that more than learning what had happened to his brother was at stake here.

"Her adoptive father's name is Paul Moore," he said as he opened his door. "He's a doctor here in Riverford and smelled human—though now I'm not so sure we can trust what our noses tell us about anyone associated with Kylie. You might want to start there."

CHAPTER FOUR

*P*aul had barely lifted a hand to knock on their friend, Karen's, front door when the door abruptly swung open and Karen waved them inside with an urgent hand before either of them could say a word.

"It's bad," the cougar shifter said grimly as she quickly shut the door behind them.

It was a testament to how frantic their friend was that she didn't bother to comment on either Kylie's state of undress or the fact that she no longer smelled like a shifter of any kind.

"I would make a joke about the Men in Black invading the city, but from what my son and some of my friends and associates have been telling me, that's not far from the truth. We were dead wrong about how many from the lion clans have managed to sneak into

Riverford."

"What are we talking about here? Sniffers? Special Ops?" Paul demanded as Kylie's heart dropped into the pit of her stomach.

"At this point, it's hard to say," Karen replied. "Mitch and a couple of his friends drove out of Riverford along the southern highway right after you called me, and he said there were a couple of SUVs parked along the right shoulder right outside the city limits with a couple of men looking under the hood of one. Nothing too suspicious there, right? Except I just got off the phone with a friend who reported seeing the exact same setup along the city's northern exit. I reported it to the Elders, but it may take a while for them to contact a few shifters on the force to send them packing."

It took every ounce of restraint Kylie had to keep from dropping the F-bomb, something she tried never to do in present company. Dammit! She had to get out of Riverford before—

"Hunter and I were attacked by a lioness this morning in the forest behind my new apartment building, so leaving by foot is definitely out of the question, too," Kylie told Karen. "She was probably one of their assassins."

Karen's eyes widened to almost comical proportions as she grabbed Kylie by the shoulders. "One of those bastards actually *saw* you?"

"And got blood on me. Unfortunately I didn't realize it at the time, and I shifted in order to help Hunter fight her off. The lioness was not amused to find a lioness siding with a jaguar. She seemed to think I was a Rogue from one of the lion clans, and I'd rather not disabuse her of that assumption."

"Then…that means your jaguar friend—"

"He wasn't very amused, either," Kylie cut her off, hating the bleak note she couldn't quite keep out of her voice.

Karen's eyes softened. "I was wondering why the only jaguar scent coming from you was faint and male. I suppose there's no reason for you to continue on pretending to be just a jaguar now that a prominent member of the jaguar clan has learned your secret. It's lucky that you inherited your father's ability."

Kylie nodded. "Being human is safer. My father always said that being able to revert back to one hundred percent human was rare even for a Polyshifter. Beyond the lion clans, I'm not even sure if that little factoid is even known. No one looking for us will look twice at a couple of humans. I'll just have to be careful to keep my face covered for those that have seen it."

"Provided we can even leave the city," Paul said. "Our best chance would be to leave the moment the shifters in the police department clear out anyone suspicious along the northern highway. I'm starting to think that maybe you shouldn't drive us after all."

"Or we can ride in the trunk for at least part of the way," Kylie offered, even though the thought of being confined in that suffocating darkness so soon after that hellish night made her mouth go dry and pulse speed up with a surge of fear.

"Absolutely not!" Paul exclaimed. "After what you've already gone through, I wouldn't ever—"

"I can't be sure that Hunter won't come after me," Kylie interrupted pointedly. "I saw it in his eyes, Paul. The suspicion, the betrayal, but most of all, the uncertainty. I've never mentioned Karen to him, but everyone at the hospital knows you two are friends. Why make it easy for him to follow our trail? It's my fault that Hunter's even in this predicament, and the last thing I want is to force him into another situation where he has to choose between me and his duty to his clan."

"Then we'll bring Mitch along, too," Karen suggested, "make it seem our trip to Dallas is just a normal family weekend outing."

"There's no need to involve your son any more than you already have," Paul said. "I would never forgive myself if something happened to him. I hate even having to ask this much of *you*."

"Like you, I swore to Alan and Grace that I would do everything in my power to keep Kylie out of the lions' hands." Karen's expression suddenly turned stern. "You don't need to do everything yourself, Paul. The same goes for you, too, Kylie. This is no time to be stubborn."

Paul crossed his arms against his chest. "All right. You both have brought up good points." He turned to Kylie. "Why don't you go upstairs and change while Karen and I hash out the finer details. Hopefully we'll have a better idea of our path forward by the time you come back."

Kylie looked down at herself and grimaced. Yeah, if Karen was going to call Mitch to join them, then she definitely didn't want him to see her barely dressed as she was.

She reached down and picked up one of the duffle bags at her feet. "I'll be right back."

Looking at the dirty and pathetic state of her feet, Kylie decided to take a quick shower. Lord knew when she would have the chance for another once they left Riverford.

After removing Hunter's jacket, she carefully folded it and stuffed it into the bag once she had taken out a pair of jeans and a simple blue blouse. She knew she should probably just chunk it into the trash. Keeping it with her would only serve to rub salt into the wound that had opened up in her heart, and right now when her mind needed to be clear and sharp, she just didn't need that particular weakness to distract her.

"You're so stupid," she muttered, her voice sounding more weary than disgusted as she had intended.

What she had shared with Hunter was over. The sooner she accepted that, the sooner the hand that was currently brutally squeezing her heart could let go.

By the time she made it back downstairs, Paul and Karen's low voices coming from the living room had been joined by a deep, energetic third.

When she stepped into the room, Karen's son, Mitch, was sitting on the couch with his back to her next to Paul listening to his mother talk about the merits of staying on the interstate versus taking the back roads. He turned before she could call out a greeting, his nostrils visibly flaring.

"Wow. You really do smell just like before," Mitch said, narrowing his eyes curiously at her as though she was a puzzle to be unraveled. Not surprising as he was an engineer. "Completely human. Not a hint of jaguar at all."

Kylie smiled thinly and walked over to him. She held out her hand to him.

"Here. Take a good, long whiff. I'd like to know if that's really true."

Mitch looked at her strangely, and she hastened to explain, "My mother always said that when my father was in his human form, he had a faint, underlying scent that gave away what he truly was, but she never described exactly what she had smelled."

Paul nodded. "Alan and I discussed it a few times. He said it was like trying to hide a natural scent with a spray of cologne. A shifter really has to stick his nose close to even realize it's there. It's the scent all Poly-shifters carry from birth until their first shift."

Mitch took Kylie's hand and lifted it up to press the back of it directly over his nose. He inhaled deeply several times before moving her hand away.

"I stand corrected," he said. "There's definitely an underlying—sweetness, for lack of a better word, beneath the normal muskiness of your human scent. However, the only reason why I even noticed it was because I was looking for it specifically. As long as someone doesn't press their nose into your skin, I think you'll be fine. You can't smell it at all in the air around you."

Karen closed her eyes and sniffed the air for several seconds. "All I smell are two humans and a kitten."

Kylie couldn't help but smile at the sour look Mitch shot his mother. She was grateful for Karen's attempt at easing some of the tension in the air.

"That's good," she said. "One less thing I have to worry about. I'll just have to be careful not to leave a sock behind anywhere. Speaking of, any updates while I was changing?"

"Nothing yet," Paul said as Mitch scooted over to make room for her on the couch. "We were just trying to decide the best route to Mobile once we've planted the false trails in Dallas. If we manage to leave River-ford before noon today and drive all night once we leave Dallas, we should be able to make a late after-noon flight tomorrow from Mobile Regional Airport to Heathrow in London."

"Nonstop?" Kylie asked hopefully.

Paul sighed. "I wish. The best I could find was a flight with a two-hour layover in Atlanta. All the rest connect to JFK, and I'd like to avoid stopping in New York City at all costs. Flying into Heathrow is enough of a risk as it is. We'll decide where to go from there on the flight over." He fixed Kylie with an intense gaze. "We have a lot to discuss first."

The invisible hand around her heart squeezed tighter. She struggled to keep the pain from her ex-pression as she nodded. Another painful conversation she had prayed they would never have to have.

She knew what she would have to do going for-ward. Now that her secret had been revealed to out-siders, her days of living out in the open as a normal human were over. She would have to say goodbye to her friends, to college. She would do all of this for Paul's sake. After everything that Paul had done to protect her, it was her turn now to protect him from a life of fear and running.

Kylie had to seek out her mother's Polyshifter clan, a place that might as well be ripped out of the pages of a fairytale for all she knew its location beyond some vague references her mother had once made to her about it being in the British Isles. More importantly, it was a place where a human could neither step foot in nor find. If she managed to find it and if they accepted her into their fold, it would be as if she had disappeared off the face of the earth.

Once Paul and she arrived in London, Kylie would have say to goodbye and go on alone.

CHAPTER FIVE

Relativity sucks, Hunter thought irritably as he stared at the unmoving man, willing him to open his eyes with every fiber of his being. However, the man's eyelids didn't so much as twitch.

A quick glance at the large, round-faced clock that hung on the wall facing the hospital bed told him that he had been sitting by the wolf shifter's bedside for only an hour when it had literally felt like days. Sitting still and doing nothing was practically torture. While he knew how important it was to be the first person the wolf saw when he finally woke up, Hunter felt completely useless, especially given the task Maxim had taken up while he sat twiddling his thumbs.

The idiot that he was, he couldn't even try calling

Kylie because his phone was currently lying somewhere in the dirt in the forest, and he couldn't remember her number. No doubt everyone under the sun was trying to call him and wondering why he wasn't picking up. He expected a barrage of phone calls to the clinic any second now.

He hoped to fuck Kylie hadn't been one of those missed calls. He also prayed that Maxim would be able to locate her before the Elders started asking about her whereabouts. He would have to tell them the truth, and right now, he wasn't a hundred percent sure that was the right thing to do. With the life of a woman he had come to care for a great deal on the line, he damned well better be one hundred percent sure.

Hunter winced at that last thought, realizing what he had been refusing to admit to himself. Why else had her very likely betrayal have pierced him so painfully rather than just stoke his anger?

He dropped his head into his hands. No matter what truth was revealed, he was utterly screwed either way.

Suddenly, a sharp gasp sounded to his left, and Hunter jerked his head up in enough time to see the wolf shifter practically leap from the bed with a snarl of warning, his blue eyes glassy with confusion and panic and darting from side to side as if frantically searching for an escape route. Hunter immediately froze in his chair, not daring to move as the man used the bed as a barricade.

The high-pitched sound of the heart monitor signaling a flatline filled his ears. Not surprising as the wolf's IV tube and finger pulse oximeter were now dangling off the edge of the bed next to him. He could both smell and see blood trickling from the back of the man's left hand where the IV needle had been ripped out.

He had to do something to calm the fear-crazed man quickly before either he tried to shift or the medical staff responding to the flatline signal made it to the room. Hunter slowly rose from his chair, immediately capturing the wolf's attention.

"Stay back! Stay back!" the wolf shouted, his voice cracking. His eyes were still wild and clearly seeing enemies everywhere. "I'll fucking bite your hands off if you so much as *reach* for me, I swear…!

Instead of wasting time with reassurances of safety that would never be believed, Hunter folded his arms against his chest and said in his most authoritative voice, "Listen, buddy. You were the one who came looking for *me* in *my territory*. We just saved your ass, so why don't you calm the fuck down before you reopen all your wounds and waste all my clansmen's efforts."

The wolf stopped snarling at him for a moment,

his eyes narrowing suspiciously for a split-second before they widened in disbelief.

· "I—remember," he rasped. "In the forest—you're Ryder's brother!"

Hearing that name made Hunter's chest tighten painfully with a maelstrom of emotions. He forced his face into a neutral expression and nodded with a calm he absolutely did not feel.

"Thank God," the wolf said, collapsing to his knees with something like a sob, letting his forehead fall against the edge of the mattress. "I thought the Retrievers had caught me."

"Retrievers?" Hunter questioned with a frown. "I had the lioness on your tail pegged as one of their assassins."

The wolf looked up sharply, a flash of fear in his eyes, before he shook his head. "No, they—"

The door abruptly burst opened and both men growled at the sudden intrusion almost in unison. Gerald, the young doctor in the forefront of the entering staff, instantly stopped after only moving a couple of strides into the room, causing the two nurses behind him to nearly collide into his back. He looked from first his would-be patient crouching in a defensive position on the other side of the bed, his hospital gown halfway open and barely covering his crotch, to the still-wailing heart monitor, to Hunter.

"Good timing," Hunter lied, struggling to keep his irritation at the interruption from his voice. "You can help him get back into bed. He was still disoriented and in danger mode when he woke up, but..." He turned his attention to the wolf. "...you're okay now, right?"

The wolf shifter stared at Hunter for a couple of seconds before slowly nodding.

Still looking a bit wary, Gerald approached the injured man as cautiously as if he was a wounded, cornered animal. After a moment's hesitation, a male nurse whose name Hunter couldn't remember followed. Once the wolf was back in his bed, Gerald picked up his bleeding hand and *tsked* after examining it more closely.

"You've definitely blown out this vein," Gerald said. "Shawn, grab some supplies to clean and bandage the wound while I examine the rest of his bandages. Sidney, I need you to start another IV in his other hand."

While the three attended to the wolf, Hunter stepped away to lean against the far wall, observing them in silence. He was dismayed to see blood seeping through one of the wolf's bandages along his back, wondering if the doctor would decide that the injured man needed rest and kick him out.

If that happened, he would have to get the Elders

involved, something he had been hoping to avoid until he'd had a chance to talk with the wolf privately. He was already walking a thin line as it was not calling Gaither the moment the wolf shifter had awakened as the Elder had requested. He couldn't afford any more delays.

"It hurts, but nothing that warrants you pumping me full of more drugs," the wolf was saying, drawing Hunter out of his thoughts. "The last thing I need right now is to be fuzzy headed and on the verge of passing out again."

"Yes, it's important that I talk to him as soon as possible," Hunter cut in, deciding a little nudge was needed. "The Elders are expecting my call."

Gerald looked over at him and frowned. "Just make it quick, Hunter. We may heal fast, but we're not immortal."

"It's okay, Doc," the wolf assured him. "He has every right. It was his territory I breached, after all."

Clever. For a jaguar, a breach of territory was the one thing others could not interfere with, not even the Elders. He would have used the excuse himself, but he felt the less everyone knew about the incident, the better. At least he was guaranteed privacy now.

Gerald sighed, but nodded. "I resealed your wound. Just try not to move any more than what's necessary. You may have only reopened one of your wounds a small bit this time, but next time you may not be so lucky. I'll be back in an hour to re-examine them."

Only when the door closed behind them did Hunter move to reclaim his seat next to the bed.

"For future reference, I would rather you not mention breaching my territory to anyone else," Hunter said.

"He wouldn't have left us alone, otherwise," the wolf replied. "What I'm about to tell you is for your ears only. Your brother seemed to think that you were our best chance, and given what he sacrificed to ensure that I had a chance to escape, I'm inclined to trust his judgment with you."

Hunter stared at him for a long moment, trying to process what this man was telling him. However, right now he only wanted to hear the answer to a single question.

"Ryder was alive when you last saw him?"

One beat, two, and then his heart began to drop to the pit of his stomach when the wolf didn't answer right away.

"He was when I last saw him," the wolf finally answered, "though from the beating he was receiving, I can't with all honesty say that's still true."

It took every ounce of will in Hunter's being to keep from shifting and going for the injured wolf's throat. *It isn't what it sounds like. He didn't run and leave Ryder behind. He wouldn't have dared come to me, otherwise.*

Over and over he repeated those thoughts in his head until he could no longer feel his muscles rippling.

Taking a final, deep breath in order to calm his lingering anger, Hunter finally fixed the wolf with what was probably still a hard gaze. "Maybe we should start at the beginning. I've never seen you running with the Riverford packs before. What's your name?"

Hunter was pleased that his tone sounded normal rather than tinged with hostility. The last thing he needed to do was to cause this man to clam up.

The wolf's body was visibly tense as he met Hunter's gaze without blinking. No doubt he had sensed how close he had come to getting his throat ripped out.

"That's because I'm from one of the suburbs— Parker Grove. My name's Jack Bray. I only have cousins here."

"So you're part of Tanner Bray's lot."

Jack's shoulders relaxed a bit as he nodded.

"Although I really would like to know how you ended up bleeding in my part of the forest, answer me this first. Were you and Ryder being held against your will by the lions?"

The look in Jack's eyes turned from wary to bleak. "We were their personal lab rats is what we were."

CHAPTER SIX

*H*unter sucked in a sharp breath. "Explain."

Jack turned his head, his gaze fixing on some point along the far wall in front of him. "About a year ago, my mate, Maya, and I were heading south out of Parker Grove to our favorite hunting spot when we were pulled over by what I thought was a highway patrol car. Two human patrolmen ordered us out of the car before I could even say a word, telling me that our license plate matched one of a suspected drug runner and they planned to search it. However, once we both had gotten out and had walked to the rear of the car where they had directed us, the sons-of-bitches Tased us, and it must have been set at a really high voltage because I blacked out almost instantly.

"I woke up as the same men—only now they were

dressed in normal jeans and t-shirts—were pulling me out of the back of an SUV parked behind a large two-story brick house. It was surrounded by cattle pens as far as the eye could see."

His face suddenly contorted into a look of disgust. "The smell was probably what woke me. It was like I'd been chucked into a lake of cow shit, it was so eye-wateringly bad. Just thinking about it now makes me want to hurl. Only when I escaped a few days ago did I find out it was a cattle ranch pretty much in the middle of nowhere, about a couple of miles west of Amarillo. At least that's what it is on the surface, but below, it's a medical research facility several floors deep right out of a horror movie."

As Jack talked, Hunter felt his body grow stiffer and stiffer with barely contained rage. It was only when his palms started to sting that he realized that his nails had started to elongate into claws and had stabbed into the pads of his tightly-fisted hands.

"Did the same thing happen to Ryder?" Hunter growled, unable to keep the anger from his voice this time.

Jack shook his head. "He said he was taken down by a tranquilizing dart while out on a run in his forest territory. I imagine it was the same one where you found me. He did say that once he had been missing for a while, you would have taken it over. We knew that all the roads leading into Riverford were being watched by the Sniffers, so that's why I aimed to get into Riverford through the forest along the southern edge. I figured if I didn't run into you within the forest, itself, then I would try looking for you at some of the places Ryder mentioned."

"Did those bastards take anyone else other than you three?"

"I only know of twelve others—all female. A couple of cougars, an alligator, a gray wolf, a tiger—"

"That tiger," Hunter cut in, nearly falling out of his chair as he unconsciously leaned closer to the wolf. "Do you know her name?"

Jack's gaze suddenly became hyper-focused. "Anna."

Hunter slowly let out the breath he had been holding. He didn't know whether or not to feel overjoyed or stricken to finally hear someone speak that name.

"Twenty-two? Blonde hair, blue eyes?" He had to make sure before…

"Yeah." Jack's voice was barely louder than a whisper. "She looked about that age, though I only saw her once, about six months ago, as we were both being dragged down a hall. It was probably when she was first brought in because boy did that tiger fight the bastards who had her with everything she had in her.

You see, once the lions' scientists get a hold of you and start pumping their shit into your veins, you're lucky to even lift a finger without breaking a sweat."

· Hunter stared at the wolf in horror for a long moment before he closed his eyes in renewed pain. "*Fuck.*"

"You're a jaguar, but—" Jack began hesitantly.

"Anna Barkova. She's my best friend's mate-to-be, not mine," Hunter finished for him. "Too many things match up for it not to be her. Just what the fuck were those bastards doing to all of you?"

The sadness and weariness on Jack's face suddenly melted into something unreadable. "Like I said, we were lab rats," he replied, his voice deepening with renewed tension. "The hell if I know what those sick bastards hoped to accomplish doing what they did to us. It was painful and debasing, and if I ever get my hands on those fuckers, I will enjoy slowly tearing out their throats!"

It was apparent that he wasn't going to get any more details other than that from the wolf, not when the horror of what he had been through was so fresh, so Hunter decided to try a different angle.

"You said that my brother helped you escape," Hunter said, watching the other man's face carefully. "How did it come about? From what you've told me, I got the impression that everyone they abducted were kept separated."

"The females at least," Jack confirmed. "Sometimes they would inject shit into me that would either force me to shift or turn me into a raging lunatic and put me in a room with Ryder or another guy—a coyote shifter—for a day or two."

A look of rage abruptly flashed in his eyes, and for a split-second, Jack was one hundred percent wolf. "I don't know the coyote's name or where he was from. By the time I met him, his human soul was completely gone. Only a scared, crazed coyote remained. I get the feeling that those lion bastards put us in there with the intention to induce us to fight. Sometimes we could resist the urge to attack, sometimes we couldn't. Afterwards, they would measure our brainwaves and draw blood…and other things."

"I can't believe you actually managed to hatch an escape plan in those kinds of conditions. No doubt you were being watched closely."

"That's just where we met each other," Jack said. "It was where we formed a bond where we knew we could trust each other. You see, sometimes we would be put in that room without the rage juice or with us both in our human forms. We would talk, mostly about random shit like hunting or football, but every so often we would reveal important stuff to each other, a word at a time.

"When we talked about hunting, he would say phrases like 'trust a hunter to,' 'Riverford's hunters are pretty tenacious,' or 'hunting with my clan brothers has saved my ass more than once.' It took me a couple of conversations to realize what he was doing. I wasn't sure if he meant a literal brother, but judging by how many times he brought up the word 'hunter' in a single conversation, I figured it was probably a name. He also exclusively mentioned the forest along Riverford's southern border as well as bitched about how there were now too many apartment complexes built right up to the forest's edge."

He smiled self-deprecatingly. "I talked about braying donkeys a lot."

Hunter almost smiled, but the atrocities being revealed made certain that he wouldn't be smiling anytime soon.

"In this way," Jack continued, "we managed to come to an understanding that if an opportunity ever opened up to escape, we would make sure at least one of us got away."

· "Hence your earlier comment about Ryder being beaten when you last saw him."

To his credit, Jack didn't look away from the steel that was probably in his eyes. "Once a month, they would bring us to the surface into an outside pen, for the sunlight, I suppose. Who knows what those sick bastards were thinking. It was surrounded by ten feet of electrified fence. Then a few days ago, a miracle happened. I happened to kick a rock at the fence and it didn't spark. Ryder threw another just to make sure the bastards weren't fucking with us—remember, everything seemed to be an experiment—but nothing happened again.

"Without the electrical current, the wire was laughably weak. We waited until a couple of the guards closest to where we were standing started talking, and I ripped a hole large enough for us to squeeze through. We transformed and made a run for it, but Ryder was shot in the leg. I don't know if it was a bullet or tranq dart, but he roared and turned back to charge the guards. As I maneuvered around the pens, the last glimpse I caught of him was in his human form on the ground being kicked by three of them.

"It took me half a week to cross the state. I stole a car in the first small town I found and drove as far southeast as Temple. I figured being so close to Riverford that traveling in wolf form and avoiding the highways was best. I made it to about a mile outside the city when that bitch found me."

He looked down at the bandages down one arm and grimaced. "As you can see, I was seriously getting my ass kicked, but luckily we tumbled towards the edge of a cliff with about a sixty foot drop. I somehow managed to shove her over. It was then that I realized how hurt I was. Frankly, I'm shocked I actually managed to drag myself so far. When I heard the female jaguar with you say your name…I was afraid that I had already passed out from the pain and blood loss, it was too good to be true. I think I was even hallucinating at that point, seeing faces from other victims. That's why I freaked out when I woke up and saw myself connected to tubes again. I was certain that Retriever or assassin or whatever she was had managed to climb back up that cliff and had found me collapsed somewhere. I hope she broke her neck and is rotting in hell right now!"

It was probably best not to tell him about his own run-in with the lioness just yet, especially when Jack's eyes now held a hint of desperation. "Do what you want with what I've told you. Tell your Elders everything, some, or nothing. Ryder believed that you could find a way to help all of us so much that he was willing to risk being killed to give me the chance to get to you."

Hunter felt a weight equal to the mass of the earth drop onto his shoulders. He closed his eyes, not wanting the other shifter to see his turmoil.

"It's because Ryder knew that only I, and our tiger friend, Maxim, are stupid enough, insane enough, to try to take on the lions head on in order to save him,"

Hunter said quietly. "Did he know about Anna?"

"I don't know. I only learned her name a few weeks ago when a couple of my tormenters were discussing the female tiger shifter over what they thought was my unconscious body. Ryder knew one of the kidnapped shifters was a female tiger, but whether or not he had ever seen her wasn't something he ever told me."

"That they mentioned her recently gives me some hope that she's still alive." Hunter opened his eyes and met Jack's eyes. "There aren't enough words in the universe to thank you for crawling through hell just to find me, but I promise you that I'll do everything possible to get our loved ones out of that cesspit even if Maxim and I have to charge in alone. In the meantime, is there anything I can do for you right now?"

"Can you bring me a phone?" Jack asked. "I need to call my father, my Elders."

"Of course."

Hunter picked up the cordless phone sitting on the nightstand beside the hospital bed from its charging base and handed it to the wolf. He then stood up.

"I'll give you some privacy. Just holler when you're done. I'll keep the doc busy if he comes before you're finished."

"Thank you."

The genuine gratitude in his voice was almost

painful to hear. As helpless as Hunter was feeling at the moment, it wasn't something he thought he deserved.

"And Hunter," Jack called out just as Hunter was opening the door. "You and Maxim won't have to go at it alone. The Parker Grove wolf clan will stand with you. I'll make sure of it."

CHAPTER SEVEN

"That pretty much sums it up," Hunter said into the phone as he stood inside one of the clinic's empty offices.

The silence on the other end of the line from Donald Gaither as he had quickly related several key facts of his discussion with Jack had almost been tangible. That the man always with a thousand questions hadn't asked a single one throughout his entire report was more than a little unnerving.

"Jack's spoken with both his family and his Elders. I imagine they'll be here to move him to one of their own facilities within the hour."

"I'm on the way as we speak," Gaither said. "Martinez, Davis, and both Alvas are waiting for my call. We should all arrive to receive them in twenty minutes or so. Is Kylie with you? Now I know you said this morning that she was stable, but I would prefer you keep her away from the Elders of another clan for the moment. We don't need another incident in this already delicate situation."

Hunter's heart sank. He had hoped that Gaither wouldn't bring Kylie up at all.

"No," he replied, careful to keep his tone as business-like as before. "Her father called after I spoke with you, and she went to have breakfast with him instead of joining me on my morning run."

"Wait—you aren't *with* her?" Gaither nearly shouted. "One of the lions' assassins is doing God-only-knows what in the city, and you left her alone with only a *human* to protect her!"

"Spare me the lecture, Gaither!" Hunter snapped. "I'm not psychic, damn it!"

"Call her," the Elder commanded in what Hunter had come to think of as his "CEO voice." Too bad that Hunter wasn't one of his employees. "Tell her you're on your way to pick her up, and for God's sake, don't let her out of your sight. She may be the lions' next target for abduction for all we know. Take her to your apartment for the time being. Once we finish meeting with the Parker Grove wolf clan Elders, we'll join you to discuss strategies for her safety."

"No way in hell you're having that meeting with

the wolves without me!" Hunter growled. "This is my brother's life we're talking about!"

"I doubt very much we will be discussing or deciding anything more than a time and place for further discussions," Gaither said dryly. "Clan members need to be warned about this new danger, intelligence gathered about the ranch the wolf spoke of. We must tread carefully, Hunter, no matter how painful it is for you to do so. For now, you can help the clan best by protecting our most vulnerable member."

An image of lioness-Kylie roaring at the other lioness flashed in his mind, and Hunter had to lock his jaw to keep from laughing. Vulnerable his ass. That was an alpha female if he ever saw one. Maybe if he had been thinking with his brain instead of his cock, he would have been able to see beyond the façade she had painted and called her bluff.

"Hunter…" Gaither's voice suddenly growled in impatience.

He only just managed not to hiss back.

Fine. If Gaither wanted to go all politician on him and dance around the issue, then Maxim and he would just have to take matters into their own hands. Ryder and Anna simply didn't have time for all the usual bullshit.

He had gotten Jack's number before he had left the poor bastard to rest, and while he did agree with

Gaither that intelligence was the next step, Maxim could have his security team and various contacts across the state on the case before any of the wolf clan Elders stepped foot in the clinic.

"You know how to find me," was all Hunter said as he ended the call before the Elder could say another word.

He quickly put in a call to Maxim. Hopefully his friend had made some progress in finding Kylie. No matter how painful, the question of her loyalty was something that absolutely had to be resolved as soon as possible. Now that the mystery of his brother and Anna's disappearance had been somewhat answered, there was too much at stake at this point to leave such a huge loose end untied. If she was a threat, she had to be dealt with, and if not... A wave of heat that had nothing to do with anger abruptly washed through him, and he nearly dropped the phone.

Christ, he was so fucked.

"Maxim, where are you?" he demanded a little more roughly than he had intended the second the call connected. "We need to talk *now*. That wolf was a treasure trove of information like you wouldn't believe."

"I'm in my office at the club. Good timing. I was just about to call you. Some major shit is going down right now in regards to Kylie, and we need to decide what to do ASAP."

Fuck. Was she really—

"Tell it to me straight, Maxim," Hunter bit out. "Is she one of those bastards?"

For a few seconds, only silence reached his ear, and he felt something tighten in his chest.

"While the jury's still out, some of the things I've found out in the last hour are pointing to no," Maxim finally replied cautiously, "but it's not something I want to discuss over the phone."

"Right. I'll be there in less than twenty."

Now to find a ride to his apartment so he could pick up his truck. He hoped to God Kylie's pheromones had faded enough overnight. The last thing he needed was her potent "come fuck me" scent mucking with his brain again.

***

"You look like you're in pain," Maxim commented the moment Hunter stepped into his office at the club.

Hunter's scowl deepened. "Let's just say that I would have been better off walking here."

His friend's nostrils flared as he neared. "I see what you mean. I'll send a couple of my men to blast the inside of your truck with ozone. Until then, I'll loan you one of mine."

Hunter collapsed into a chair. "Thanks. I have a feeling I'll be needed it a lot today." He then fixed Maxim with a serious gaze. "Maxim, that wolf saw Ryder and Anna."

Maxim had been leaning back in his chair in his usual casual sprawl, but at Hunter's words, he sprang forward so quickly, a wild look in his eyes, that for a split-second he thought Maxim was about to lunge over the desk at him.

"When? Where?" his friend demanded. The desperately hopeful look in those pale blue eyes was heartbreaking.

"It's not good. The lions have them, as we thought."

Then slowly, excruciatingly, Hunter recounted everything Jack had told him. The more he talked, the more Maxim's expression hardened until the tiger's anger was all he could smell. He had been anxious to get rid of the smell of Kylie's heat from his nose, but not like this. The sharp smell of Maxim's anger was so strong, the look in his eyes so feral, that Hunter feared his friend was about to lose control of his tiger.

Then Maxim abruptly slammed both fists onto the top of his desk, making Hunter involuntarily hiss in reaction, and he realized just how much on edge he, himself, had become as he had talked.

"I'm going to shred every inch of flesh from those

bastards' bodies before ripping open their bellies with my fangs," Maxim snarled, his voice so deep and full of rage that he sounded like a stranger.

In the twenty plus years he had known the tiger shifter before him, Hunter had never seen him even close to this pissed off.

"We will," Hunter assured him just as fiercely. "Jack has promised the help of his clan, and I believe him."

From the pinched expression on his face, Hunter could tell Maxim was putting tremendous effort into reigning in his fury. Maxim had always been the mellower of the two, which was saying a lot given Hunter's general aloofness, and he was grateful for it. Now, more than ever, they would need his friend's levelheadedness.

Maxim closed his eyes and drew in a final, calming breath before he said, "The wolf clans are the best allies one can have, so at least there is a sliver of good news in all that horror."

"A few of my Elders will be meeting with the Parker Grove wolf clan Elders and Jack's pack shortly. I wanted to stay for it, gather as much information before dropping such a huge bomb on you, but then Gaither brought up Kylie."

Maxim nodded and sat back in his chair, though the rigidness in his body remained. "Given that you actually fought a shifted lion inside Riverford, I'm not surprised she was his main priority. Historically, clans have always acted a little crazy whenever a Returner popped up."

"But is she *really* a Returner?" Hunter asked, his uncertainty bleeding into his tone. "When she confessed to me that she knew she was a Polyshifter, she also called herself a Returner. After lying to all of us about her ignorance, how can we ever trust anything she says or has said?" *For all I know, getting me to fall for her was all part of some nefarious plan.*

"Which brings us to the 'serious shit going down' I warned you about earlier. While my people were talking to the staff at Riverford Regional, a certain suspected Sniffer was also seen talking to a couple of nurses. Like us, the man was asking about Kylie's father, how they might be able to reach him. Luckily those nurses knew no more about Dr. Moore other than that he was one of the hospital's rotating doctors rather than on permanent staff. I think my people spooked him because he ran off soon after, but the fact that a Sniffer was asking about someone close to Kylie could mean several things."

"A misdirection," Hunter couldn't help saying. "Planting doubt to any suspicions."

Maxim nodded. "Lord knows how those bastards

plan to come at us. That they've been quietly and successfully kidnapping shifters in our area is likely just the tip of the iceberg. Maybe their plan was to use Kylie as a distraction, something that would undoubtedly draw our eyes momentarily away from what we should have been doing."

Hunter narrowed his eyes. "But you don't think that's it. You said as much when I flat-out asked."

Maxim smiled thinly. "I don't, but only because I found out that Dr. Moore has been good friends with a cougar-shifter RN named Karen Wilson and her son for years and that she called in sick to the hospital this morning. If not for that fact, I imagine my suspicion would have run deeper than even yours."

Hunter frowned. "I don't know any Wilsons personally."

"Sasha's husband has been friends with Karen's son, Mitch, since they were brats barely able to shift. Although I don't know the particulars, I do know that Karen's husband was killed by a couple of lions on a business trip to New York when Mitch was only three, so there's no way in hell that family is associated with the lions. If they're the ones either hiding or trying to get Kylie and her dad out of Riverford, then I have a hard time believing that Kylie is one of the lions' pet Polyshifters simply for the fact that Karen, more than anyone else, would have been suspicious of a human girl suddenly shifting for the first time in adulthood.

"However, despite all of that, we're really just flying in the dark right now. You need to get over to the Wilson house right now, and if Kylie is indeed there, start convincing her and her dad that they need to leave with you."

"I think I'm the last person she would want to see right now," Hunter protested, "especially with the way I blew her off earlier when she tried to explain herself."

Maxim shook his head. "Right now, you're probably the only shifter she would even agree to talk to, much less let anywhere near her."

Hunter ran a hand through his hair in agitation. "I'll try, but don't be surprised if she attacks me instead. I don't want to hurt her, but she may not give me a choice."

"Hmm—good point." Maxim grabbed his cell phone from his desktop and began scrolling through his contacts. "Maybe a surprise visit isn't the best way to go about this. Sasha sent me Mitch's number earlier just in case. Maybe if we alert them to the danger, tell them we know Kylie's an innocent in all this and that we believe the lions are coming for her, they may agree to accept our help. For this, I think it's best that we deal with Mitch rather than his mother."

"Send him a text first," Hunter said. "Tell him you

need to talk to him about something important but to make sure he's not overheard by anyone, especially his mother. That way, if Kylie and her father really are with them, they won't be spooked into running again."

"I can do one better," Maxim said. "The Wilsons live clear across town in The Highlands residential area. It should take you a good thirty minutes to get there. After he responds to the text, *if* he responds, then you leave here, and I'll wait about twenty minutes to make that follow-up call. That way if they do choose to run, you'll be close enough to maybe head them off, though I sincerely hope it doesn't come to that. If she's there and she agrees to talk, then send me a text. I'll gather some of my security and meet you there. We can all decide what to do from there."

"Maxim—once you talk with Mitch, I really do think you should let me deal with the rest alone. You should be concentrating on gathering intel on that ranch. We both know that you and your people have the best chance of unearthing something useful."

"And that's exactly what I'm doing. As a Poly-shifter, Kylie may very well have information vital to our cause, but if it turns out Kylie hid her true heritage out of fear rather than subterfuge, then she may be the very key we need to successfully infiltrate that ranch of horrors."

"That's a lot of ifs," Hunter said.

"After months of a whole lot of nothing, suddenly within a few hours today, you've talked to a guy who has seen Anna and Ryder alive as well as learned of someone who is uniquely able to help us save them should she choose to do so," Maxim said. "Right now I'm willing to take a few things on faith that it'll all work out favorably in the end for all of us."

"Fucking optimist," Hunter quipped, shaking his head. "All right. Send your text. Let's get this show started."

CHAPTER EIGHT

Kylie nearly jumped out of her skin when Mitch's cell literally started barking.

He flashed her a sheepish grin. "Sorry. I set it as my new tone for incoming texts to tease one of my wolf friends."

"News?" Karen asked as he glanced down at his screen.

He shook his head slowly, his lips curving down slightly. "No, I don't think so. It's probably something work related. Excuse me for a moment."

Karen snorted as soon as Mitch was out of sight, making Kylie turn to look at her questioningly.

"I very much doubt that text was from a coworker," Karen said wryly. "I'd be willing to bet a year's salary that text was from his not-as-secret-as-he-thinks girlfriend."

"Ah," Paul said with a smile. "The infamous tigress."

"What tigress?" Kylie asked, eager for a distraction from her heavy thoughts.

"Lately our Elders have been a bit vocal about the younger generation's choice of mates," Karen explained. "It seems they feel too many of our newly-turned adults have been choosing non-cougar mates and are worried about our numbers dwindling. In response, the younger generations have just become more secretive about their out-of-clan relationships in order to avoid drawing the Elders' attention. Mitch knows I could care less if he's dating someone other than a cougar, but I think he's trying to avoid putting me in an awkward position with the Elders over it. I'm supposed to be encouraging him to marry a nice, sweet cougar after all."

Kylie shook her head. "The Elders do know this is the twenty-first century not the sixteenth, right?"

"From what you've told me about your meeting with the jaguar clan Elders," Paul said, "that may indeed be the problem. Perhaps the old shifter clan traditions are too ingrained to change so easily. I think—"

"We have to leave *now!*" Mitch suddenly shouted as he ran into the living room, his phone still clutched tightly in his right hand.

Kylie was immediately on her feet. "Why? What happened?"

"They know you're here! Grab your bags and let's go!"

"The lions? The jaguars? Who?" Paul demanded

"Both," Mitch replied grimly, "but right now it's the jaguars whom we have to worry about. I just got off the phone with Maxim Clarke, a prominent figure in the Siberian clan."

Kylie froze at the mention of that name. If *he* was calling then…

"He said that his people have evidence that the Sniffers have found out Kylie's identity," Mitch continued, "that he knew we were helping you two after the incident in the forest this morning." His eyes turned worriedly to Kylie. "He said that Hunter Rivera is on his way to collect you before the lions can."

Kylie felt as though she had been stabbed in the heart. Why—when she had already resigned herself to never seeing him again—why the hell did this have to happen now when she was so close to leaving Riverford for good?

She grabbed Paul's empty hand and started tugging him towards the kitchen where the door to the garage was located. "Mitch is right. We have to go *right now*."

"Kylie…!" Paul protested, planting his feet and tugging back firmly on her hand until she was forced to stop.

"No," Kylie said heatedly. "Hunter had his chance to hear me out, and he blew it. I don't know what game he and Maxim are playing, but I've made my decision. The best thing for me to do right now is to leave and go to London as we planned."

"Kylie, look at me," Paul said, dropping both her hand and the two bags he was carrying to grasp her shoulders firmly.

Kylie reluctantly met his eyes.

"Are you one hundred percent sure this is what you want to do?" he asked. "I know you're scared and hurting, but after we leave here, there's no coming back. Are you sure that's what you want? It's still not too late to change your mind. If you decide you want to wait for him, then that's what we'll do."

What I want is for us to be safe, she thought sadly, but if it was true that the lions now knew who she was and with Hunter's motives for coming after her still up in the air, safe was the last thing she would ever be if she stayed.

So she squared her shoulders and fixed him with a determined gaze. "I'm sure. Let's go."

For a brief moment, Paul looked almost stricken, but before she could even process the implications, one of the living room windows suddenly exploded inward. A figure dressed all in black and what looked like a swat vest came flying through the heavy navy curtains and came to a rest in a defensive crouch only a couple of feet from Paul's back.

Paul instinctually shoved Kylie back and started to turn when the black-clad figure slashed at his middle with a partially-shifted hand sporting the razor-sharp claws and golden fur of a lion.

"Paul!" Kylie screamed as the claws ripped through the thick material of his sport coat on his right side.

Her adoptive father grunted in surprised pain as he completed the turn and stumbled back, grabbing for his side. A dark stain was already beginning to spread out into the material beneath his hand.

"Covering yourself with human stench is clever, I'll give you that, but it's useless against me," a familiar female voice sneered, and Kylie suddenly found herself looking into the face of the lioness she had faced off against only a few hours earlier. "I got a good look at your face, and I never forget a traitor. A traitor always faces her Alpha on my watch."

Some deep instinct buried within her psyche had Kylie baring her teeth threateningly at the other woman. Then twin snarls sounded in the air behind her, and in a blur of gold, Mitch suddenly lunged past her in his cougar form towards the lioness.

The lioness shifter snarled and skillfully side-stepped his charge. Mitch attempted to stop his forward momentum and slipped on the hardwood as he was turning, crashing into the far wall. The impact caused shards of glass to rain down onto his body that had not yet fallen from the ruined window.

Kylie used the lioness's momentary distraction to race over to Paul. Her hands pressed at his back in an attempt to steady him as he backpedaled away from the fight.

"It's just a scratch," he insisted in a strained voice as Kylie frantically pulled him back.

Then suddenly there was another cougar running to stand between them, roaring warningly at their blonde attacker just as Mitch managed to right himself with a hard shake, sending a multitude of glass fragments flying in every direction.

The lioness's eyes flitted quickly between the two cougars before her eyes narrowed, and she said in a voice that demanded obedience, "Walk away. My business here is with the traitor of our clan, alone."

In answer, Mitch lunged at her back—only to fall prey to a direct kick to the muzzle that was so fast that Kylie almost didn't see the transitional movement at all. There was a sickening crack, followed by a squeal of pain, as Mitch's head snapped to the side while the rest of his body went tumbling.

Karen let out a roar of rage and leapt for the woman's throat. The lioness threw herself back with all the grace of a professional tumbler, one boot catching the underside of Karen's muzzle hard as her body bent into a back handspring. Karen dropped to the floor hard in a heap of twitching limbs, shaking her head vigorously as though trying to clear water from her ears.

"Never mind me, just run, Kylie!" Paul cried, trying to push her towards the kitchen, but there was no way in hell that was going to happen.

While Karen was only momentarily stunned, Mitch was out for the count, still in his cougar form and lying on his side about three feet from the lioness. Kylie's eyes zeroed in on the blood dripping from his muzzle.

Even if she had wanted to run, she could well imagine the lioness completing her shift and chasing after her like a lion running down a gazelle. She wasn't about to let Paul, Mitch, or Karen become that gazelle, either. No, the only chance they had left, however remote, was for her to shift and fight.

The only problem was all of her shifter souls were completely dormant at the moment. She had to somehow touch Mitch's blood before the lioness could grab her and hope she actually had a cougar soul to awaken.

Kylie had a momentary surge of irritation about the lost bracelet that she desperately needed before she abruptly broke away from Paul, causing him to topple onto his knees with a startled gasp without her support, and sprinted towards Mitch. She sensed more than saw the lioness move towards her just as she stretched out a hand and dove for the small puddle of blood. Just as her stomach hit the hardwood, she managed to dip the tips of her fingers into the liquid crimson a split-second before the back of her blouse was gripped in a tight fist and she was hauled roughly up to her knees.

She gasped, and the unique smell of lion as only a shifter could experience inundated her senses. Rather than feel a surge of triumph that her shifter side was once again active, the accompanying smell of the lioness's anger and disgust were so strong to Kylie's newly sensitive nose that all she could feel was a sudden urge to gag.

"Disgusting! I can smell this one on you, too!" her captor spat. "You're so saturated in his stink and the jaguar's that I can barely smell the lion! Not only a traitor but a whore!"

Kylie half-expected to feel the woman spit on her. Instead, the sharp tips of several claws suddenly dug into the soft flesh of her throat just short of breaking skin.

"I should just kill you now, but watching your Alpha shred you to pieces for your disgrace will be much more satisfying, I think."

It was then that the implications of the woman's earlier words finally sunk in. *She still thinks I'm a lion.*

Instead of coming to the obvious conclusion, her disgust at Kylie for sleeping with a shifter of another clan blinded her to the truth. If she shifted now, then there would be no hiding her Polyshifter heritage anymore, but if she didn't—dammit!

Her eyes darted wildly to Paul, who was still on his knees where he had fallen with an alarming amount of blood staining his side. They were screwed either way, so unless the neighbors had heard all the roaring and crashing and had called the police, then she had no choice but to—

Suddenly, what felt like a brick wall slammed into Kylie's side, and both she and the lioness went flying, landing painfully into a tangle of limbs. As she gasped and choked after a breath that was no longer there, Kylie struggled to make sense of the chaos that had abruptly erupted all around her. Hands were grabbing her beneath her armpits and dragging her back quickly across the floor, while her ears were suddenly filled with a cacophony of snarls and hisses and the smell of fresh blood reached her nostrils along with…

Kylie nearly choked again as she tilted her head

back sharply in order to confirm with her eyes what her nose was impossibly telling her. It was Hunter, his hazel eyes bright and glaring in the direction of the snarls as his face hovered above hers. A burst of conflicting emotions flooded her entire being and she immediately began struggling to pull out of his grip.

. He had sent her away. She had decided to accept it and move on. He wasn't supposed to be here, dammit!

"Don't," Hunter scolded, his gaze moving down to lock onto her own as he pulled her up until her back was pressed firmly against his chest and his arms wrapped more securely across her chest and waist.

She felt her chest tighten painfully as that word reminded her of that first show of his distrust back in the forest.

His eyes were unreadable as he added, "Let Maxim and Lana take care of that bitch."

Kylie's eyes unwittingly moved towards the fight. The lioness was currently trying to tear out the throat of a ruddy-colored wolf while the largest tiger she had ever seen had mounted her back and had one of her shoulders in a death-bite. The wolf hastily rolled away from those snapping fangs, and the lioness took advantage of that short reprieve to literally rip herself out of the tiger's jaws and bound off towards the couch and over the back.

Hunter's arms tightened around her as the lioness turned around as if to begin another charge, but then that golden, blood-speckled back suddenly began to ripple. Kylie sucked in a sharp breath when the lioness shifted back into the blonde woman.

"It's a fucking petting zoo in here!" the lioness snarled before spitting out a glob of blood onto the sofa cushions that had streamed into her mouth from the set of deep gashes Maxim had likely sliced across her forehead.

She also was bleeding from several bite wounds on an arm as well as the huge chunk of flesh missing from her right shoulder. Though she was in her human form, her posture and the way she was glaring at each of them in turn was blatantly like that of an injured, cornered animal.

For a long, tense moment that seemed to last an eternity, no one dared breathe. Then between one blink and the next, Maxim suddenly bounded forward and leapt at her, his paws hitting her squarely on the chest before she could even react, and over she went, the back of her head hitting the floor with a sickening *thunk*. He stood over the still body for a few moments, his keen eyes fixed on her face, before he stepped off to the side and shifted back into a man.

"Lana," Maxim said without taking his eyes off her, "there should be some zip ties in the back of the

SUV. They'll do for now."

A naked brunette abruptly stepped into Kylie's peripheral. "On it," she said simply before turning to head towards the front door, seemingly unconcerned that she was about to walk outside in the buff and possibly give the neighbors an eyeful.

"Keep an eye out," Hunter added. "There may be more of those bastards waiting to ambush us outside."

"Let me go!" Kylie demanded, pushing hard against his steel-like arms. "I need to get to Paul!"

She had been expecting him to resist, so she was thrown a bit off balance when he immediately loosened his arms around her. Without a word, she moved from his embrace and crawled over to where Paul was currently lying on his back, his hands pressing a wad of his own sport coat against his wound. His face was ashen, and an alarming amount of blood was starting to pool beneath him.

"Oh my God, Paul!" Kylie cried. "A scratch my ass—let me see!"

"I honestly—didn't think it was that deep," he whispered, his eyes fluttering as though he was struggling to stay conscious.

"Don't pass out on me, dammit!" Kylie barked as she moved his hands away from the wound.

A gush of blood flowed from at least three vertical slashes starting from just below his ribs and curving to his side. She hastily pressed his already blood-soaked coat hard onto the wound, making him grunt with pain. He was in very real danger of bleeding out.

"Help me! He needs an ambulance *now!*" Kylie shouted, turning pleading eyes on Hunter.

At that moment, she didn't care that this man had hurt her or about his motives for showing up at the house. The only thing that mattered was getting Paul help before he bled out right in front of her eyes. She would never forgive herself if he ended up dying because he had tried to stand between her and a lion assassin.

Kylie almost let out a sob of relief when Hunter immediately nodded.

"Leave that lion bitch to Lana," Hunter said to Maxim. "I need your help carrying him out to the truck. It would be faster if I just drive him myself rather than wait for the medics to show up."

"To your clan's clinic?" Maxim asked as he rose from his crouch. "They won't be pleased that you're taking a human there."

"I know. That's why I'm not asking first. He's lost too much blood. On top of the shock, he doesn't have time for the usual bullshit."

Lana returned, fully clothed, with the aforementioned zip ties as well as a roll of duct tape and a stack of clothes for Maxim.

"We'll stay behind and watch her as well," Karen said.

The older woman was currently sitting on the floor examining the inside of a now-conscious Mitch's mouth.

He still had a couple of trails of drying blood leading from his mouth and down his chin and a swollen lower lip. Kylie instantly felt guilty. In all the excitement and her worry for Paul, she had forgotten completely about the other two.

"Are you okay, Mitch?" Kylie asked anxiously, remembering hearing a crack at some point.

"Jus a fat rip an a itten tongue," Mitch slurred with a dismissive wave.

"Don't you worry about us Kylie," Karen said firmly. "We'll take care of things here. You just focus on your dad."

CHAPTER NINE

$\mathcal{K}$ ylie sat at her father's bedside, holding one limp and clammy hand between both of hers and listening to the steady beep of his heart monitor. They had just brought him into this private room from surgery twenty minutes ago, the lioness's claws having gone deep enough to nick the corner of his liver.

She had sat alone in the waiting room throughout the surgery, her worry and self-beratement interrupted only by the occasional update from the nurse and a call from Karen. She had been escorted there by Hunter, and after she refused to talk to him until after the surgery was over, he agreed to leave her to her lone vigil.

Although most of her attention was focused on Paul's sleeping face, Kylie could feel the presence of the silent figure leaning against the wall beside the door as keenly as if his body was pressed firmly against her back.

"I'm an asshole," Hunter abruptly said, breaking the tense silence.

Kylie stilled. Of all the things she thought he would say, *that* hadn't even entered her realm of possibilities.

"Yes, because only an asshole would save my father's life," she replied stiffly without turning around.

"You know what I mean."

If anything, she became even more rigid. When Kylie had given him her ultimatum hours earlier, she had never imagined their inevitable conversation would begin like this. He was supposed to demand answers. He was supposed to be cold. Her heart clenched. He wasn't supposed to apologize, dammit!

When she remained silent, Hunter said, "I—we just want to talk. Okay?"

His tone was neutral, giving no hints to what he was thinking. It made Kylie more nervous than she wanted to admit.

"We?" she asked with an edge to her voice.

"Don't worry. Only Maxim and I know about your true heritage. He's waiting outside the door right now."

Kylie finally turned around and fixed Hunter with a hard stare, trying to ignore the way her heart skipped a beat now that she was allowing herself to look at his face properly. One look and her heart was already betraying her. This was bad.

"You didn't even tell Mr. Gaither?"

"Only Maxim. I—the way I behaved—it was obvious that my judgment was too questionable to leave something so potentially dangerous in my hands alone," he admitted.

Kylie blinked at him in surprise, not expecting such honesty right out of the gate. First an apology and now this. What exactly was he playing at?

"And what do you think now?" she asked before she could stop herself.

Idiot! You've been down this road before, and look where it's gotten you. You already know what you have to do. You absolutely can't lose your focus now thinking about all the maybes!

"That's what Maxim's here to answer, if you'll let him," Hunter finally replied after studying her for a long, tense moment.

His answer gave her pause. It was true that this whole mess started because she hadn't been honest with him, even when Hunter had proven that he was more than trustworthy and their relationship had grown from wary friendship to something much more intimate. Yet, the fear of what her Polyshifter heritage represented to the shifter clans was ingrained in her so deeply that she wondered if it was even possible to ever lose it completely.

Maybe he was right. Maybe the best thing to have here was someone who would consider her words a little more objectively. That way, if she pleaded her case just so, then maybe Paul and she still had a chance of continuing on with their original plan of fleeing to London once he was healed.

It seemed that Hunter wouldn't be so quick to judge her on the clans' past prejudices about her people this time, and she was disturbed to find that the thought soothed the wounded part of her that still cared for him.

Despite her rising discomfort, Kylie did her best to erase the wariness from her expression. She could do this.

"Okay."

Some of the tension in Hunter's shoulders eased, making her wonder what he would have done if she'd said no and glad she would never have to find out.

Hunter reached over and lightly rapped on the door three times. The door immediately opened, and Maxim slowly, cautiously, stepped in, his body language like a cat entering potentially hostile territory. His nostrils flared as his eyes darted quickly from her to Hunter before he flashed her a tentative smile.

"So you're a 'human' this time."

Kylie stiffened briefly before she nodded towards the tiger shifter in acknowledgment. She had dipped a finger briefly in Paul's mouth on the way over, figuring that it was better to smell like a human rather than a cougar. If she had stepped foot inside the clinic smelling like a cougar then there would have been no hiding that she was a Polyshifter. At least if she smelled human, she could explain it away as a Returner thing, a reversion brought on by all the stress. It had been an extreme amount of stress that had caused her awakening, after all.

She waved a surprisingly steady hand towards the two empty chairs next to hers. "You should sit. It's been a long day, and I have a feeling it's about to get even longer."

"I'm sorry to make you do this now," Maxim began. "Hunter wanted to wait until tomorrow when you've had some time to rest or at the very least, your father had woken up from the anesthesia, but things have gone too much to shit today that time is a luxury we no longer have. We just need to be *sure*—for everyone's sake."

Kylie's eyes inadvertently flickered over to Hunter, but his expression was still as unreadable as before.

She nodded, and then took a deep breath to steady her nerves. She had a fleeting thought of her father, wondering if he had felt this anxious when he had first revealed himself to Paul.

"I've lived in fear my entire life of being discovered. You see, my birth parents are both Polyshifters, from two different clans, in fact."

"Two different clans…" Hunter repeated, his tone startled. "I thought the Polyshifter clans had all been either destroyed, scattered, or—"

"—enslaved?" Kylie finished for him, unable to keep the bitterness and anger from her voice.

Hunter and Maxim exchanged a heavy look before Hunter fixed his eyes back on her. "That night in the forest when we first crossed paths—for a moment, I smelled two humans." He looked at her expectantly.

Kylie frowned. "What are you trying to ask me?"

"You were *human*," Hunter emphasized. "I had never heard that a Polyshifter could become fully human."

"Not many of us can," Kylie admitted, "but that's not why you smelled two humans that night."

Hunter's eyes narrowed. "What do you mean?"

"You smelled two humans because before that sicko abducted me, I was one hundred percent a Deadend. I wasn't lying when I told you this earlier this morning."

Silence. Then both men began talking at once, and Kylie held up a hand sharply. "Wait! Let me finish.

Why do you think I've managed to avoid notice for *twenty years*? I was a Deadend living *with a human*. How many times does a shifter even look twice at a human crossing their path? However, that wasn't even the best part of my protection. After all, what better way to protect a Polyshifter child, even a Deadend one, if no one knows that the child exists in the first place?"

Maxim abruptly leaned forward. "Is Paul Moore really human?"

"He is," she confirmed, willing them both to see the truth in her eyes. "I know what you're thinking, but Paul really is just my adoptive father. Paul and his wife, Laura, met my parents while they were all in medical school."

"Where is she now?" Maxim asked. "Should we have called her?"

"She died of a brain aneurism a while back," Kylie replied softly.

"Oh, sorry," Maxim said, shifting uncomfortably.

"So your real parents decided to hide you with a human couple?" Hunter asked. When she nodded, he shook his head, looking perplexed. "Why didn't they just go back to live within one of the Polyshifter communities? If those clans managed to keep themselves hidden even in the Age of the Cyber Snoops, then I would think there would be no place safer for you. Hell, why did they even leave in the first place?"

Kylie sighed. "It makes sense if you know some of the Polyshifters' history as well as my parents' history. Understandably, both my father and mother's clans lived within isolated, self-sustaining—villages for lack of a better word. It's only within the past thirty, forty years that some of the Polyshifter clans have allowed their kids to go out into the world in order to attend college, not only to modernize, but to search for other Polyshifters in the hopes of widening the gene pool.

"My parents met as college freshman, and my mother soon realized that the 'human' she had befriended was a Polyshifter the first time she got a good whiff of my father's skin. You see, we Polyshifters have a unique scent that gives us away to shifters when we're masquerading as human, but it's hard to detect unless you know what to look for."

"But if they were in a completely human form, then how could your mother even pick up this scent?" Maxim asked. "Or does a Polyshifter retain the heightened senses of a shifter even when they're in a completely human state?"

"No, you're right. The enhanced senses do disappear when we're completely human. My mother, on the other hand, wasn't one of the Polyshifters that could become fully human. Though it was more dangerous for my father, because of this, once they'd graduated and married, to avoid scrutiny, they made the choice to attend med school as cougars. They all even did their residency at the same hospital. Then one night when everyone had been drinking more heavily than usual, Paul let slip to my father that he used to play with a wolf shifter kid back when he was in elementary school. Thinking that having a human friend in the know might come in handy, my father took Paul into his confidence about not only being a shifter, but a Polyshifter and why that was significant.

"By the time my mother became pregnant with me, the lions had somehow discovered my father's clan in a remote part of Canada, killing all but the youngest children."

Hunter growled, his lips twisted in disgust. "The ones that could still be molded."

Anger surged potently throughout her body until she began to tremble with it as it always did when she thought of the fate of her father's clan. "They've been hunting Polyshifters like my father, those who had been away from the village when it was attacked, ever since. With the lions now breathing down their necks, my parents went into hiding."

She smiled thinly at Hunter. "Like you, my father knew that the only place we had a chance to be safe was among my mother's clan, and he pleaded with my mother to take me and go. She flat-out refused. I think she'd had a falling out with both her Elders and parents and had left without permission. Because of that, she didn't think they would accept my father, and she didn't want to leave him behind.

"When I was eight, my parents were forced to leave me with Paul and Laura. Both Sniffers and one of the lions' assassins were close on our heels, and they were desperate to keep them from knowing that they'd had a child. They promised to come back once they were certain they'd shaken their tail but then soon after seemingly dropped off the face of the earth. Paul and Laura adopted me. We moved to Riverford, and we've been trying to find out what happened to my parents ever since."

"It's no wonder you were so interested in what I could tell you about the lion clans," Hunter said.

"Yeah." Kylie paused, and then added hesitantly, "That's why Paul and I didn't make a run for it after I became a Returner. It had been over a year since we'd discovered anything like a clue, and Paul thought well of Riverford's jaguar clan. He thought maybe you, like Karen and the cougar clan, might be able to help us someday, and the thought of belonging to a community for the first time…"

Kylie trailed off, suddenly unsure if she should have revealed that kind of weakness at this point of the game.

Hunter's eyes were suddenly golden pools of intensity. "Then—you were planning to tell me eventually?"

"Despite how much trouble I caused you, you bent over backwards to help me without batting an eye. I thought maybe, just maybe I had found someone within the shifter community that I could someday trust with this horrible secret, a friend around my age who could understand me at my core better than my human friends because it was a core we shared. I never expected—"

She looked down at her hands and swallowed against the huge lump that had suddenly formed in her throat. "I never expected last night," she finished softly.

"And that's my cue to leave," Maxim cut in dryly. He stood and looked at each of them with a hint of amusement. "I think the rest you two need to sort out alone."

Then before either one of them could say a word, he hurried out of the room, leaving Kylie and Hunter to choke on an atmosphere that had suddenly become unbelievably thick with tension.

CHAPTER TEN

"Thanks a lot, buddy," Hunter muttered under his breath as he raked a hand through his hair in agitation. "Though I suppose he has a point. The last hour has shown me just how much I let my hatred of those lion bastards fuck up my common sense. After what we shared, I should have at least had the decency to hear you out."

"Sooner or later, Polyshifters always cause chaos," Kylie whispered, still unable to look at him. "My mother used to say this all the time. Her voice always sounded so sad. It used to scare me a lot because normally she was always so incredibly cheerful and full of life. This morning proved she was right."

Kylie forced herself to look up, to capture and hold his gaze. What she said next was the hardest thing she had ever had to say, every word shattering the last of the small hope of the possibility of love she just now realized she had been clinging to by tooth and nails despite everything.

"Last night should have never happened."

Her words hung in the air like a toxic cloud ready to suffocate her. Yet, Hunter didn't so much as blink as he looked back at her with that same unreadable expression he had held before as he had stood in the back of the room staring at her back. One minute, two, then five, and the silence that had fallen between them still stretched on, broken only by the steady beeps of Paul's heart monitor, until Kylie had to struggle hard not to look away.

Then Hunter's eyes inexplicably softened. "I can see it in your eyes, you know," he said finally, "that you really believe that, but not for the reason you want me to think. You want to run, and I can understand that given everything that's happened, my fuck-up playing a not-so-insignificant part."

Kylie looked away, then lowered her eyes to Paul's still-sleeping face. "You don't need to keep apologizing. I wasn't exactly a complete innocent in all this."

She could feel Hunter's eyes boring into the back of her head, making some deep remnant of her shifter side still present in her psyche want to turn around and snap her jaws at him.

"He's going to need some time to recover," Hunter said. "In the meantime, my clan can protect him here." He was gazing intensely at her when she reluctantly turned back to him. "And I'll protect you, if you'll let me."

Kylie's heart clenched. "Please don't say that," she said softly. "Don't make this harder than it has to be. You've already seen what having a Polyshifter suddenly pop up in front of you can do to upset what you thought were strong ties. Even if the lions haven't found out about my true heritage yet, I have no doubt that assassin told others about me."

Kylie laughed humorlessly. "The rogue lion. That's almost as bad as being a Polyshifter. I don't think they'll ever stop coming after me. That's why it's better for me to leave now before things become much worse. Paul almost died this time trying to protect me. The next time he might not be so lucky to survive—or it might even be *you* that's killed—"

Hunter was out of his chair in an instant, and then his mouth, hard and demanding, abruptly silenced the rest of her words. One hand held the back of her head in place and the other snaked around her middle in order to draw her up out of her chair and flush against him. Kylie let out a muffled sound of shock and tried to pull away, but Hunter's arm was all curved steel.

Then she found her mouth opening for him of its

own accord, and suddenly his hot tongue was sliding sensually against her own.

Idiot! Idiot! she berated herself, but she couldn't bring herself to fight against the kiss seriously, especially when it was something her wounded soul wanted so badly.

The warmth of Hunter's firm body acted like a balm, and soon Kylie was closing her eyes and wrapping her arms around his waist, all but melting against him.

Hunter made a noise of pleasure against her lips, and the kiss deepened to something more frenzied and passionate.

"It seems I missed quite a lot," a raspy, amused voice suddenly broke through the loud drumming of her heart what could have been equally minutes or hours later.

Kylie immediately broke away from the kiss, feeling a surge of both guilt and joy and looked down at the mildly smiling man with the oxygen tubes up his nose. "Paul! You're awake!"

Hunter reluctantly released her when she pushed hard against his arms, but he stayed close as she carefully picked up Paul's right hand and gave it a gentle squeeze between her own.

"So I take it, it really wasn't a scratch?" Paul said more jovially than a man waking up from surgery should have been capable of, his gaze weakly sweeping the room.

Kylie fought hard to keep the tears that were threatening to well up at bay. The last thing she wanted to do was to make Paul worry about her distress.

"When is it ever?" Kylie scolded, forcing a tiny smile. "That bitch nicked your liver. Needless to say, you're going to be in here a while."

"Where are we?" Paul asked, wincing as he tried to shift his legs. "This room doesn't look like any of the patient rooms in Riverford Regional or St. Mary's."

"It's the jaguar clan's private clinic," Hunter interjected. "None of the humans even know it exists. I'm sure you, of all people, understand the need for that level of discretion in this case."

Paul's eyes narrowed. "Given the eyeful I got when I woke up, I think introductions are long overdue."

Without batting an eye, Hunter offered Paul his hand. "Hunter Rivera."

She had no idea how the bastard could handle everything so calmly all the time.

"Paul Moore. I was conscious long enough to know it was you and your people who saved my daughter from that lioness. I can't thank you enough. However, forgive me if I'm just a little bit concerned about you two starting something again given the circumstances."

Kylie winced. She heard Paul's chastisement loud and clear even if Hunter didn't. What she had just allowed to happen was incredibly dumb—no, it was actually incredibly cruel to both of them. It was just as she'd told Hunter earlier. It was simply too dangerous to stay in Riverford longer than was absolutely necessary. She knew it, and Paul knew it.

"I will protect her."

Kylie turned her head to look at Hunter so sharply that her neck cracked. What the hell was he *saying?*

But Hunter wasn't looking at her. He was looking down at Paul with a look of challenge in his eyes. Paul met his gaze with an unconscious upward lift of his chin.

An eternity later, her adoptive father slowly nodded. "As long as you truly mean it, and it's what Kylie wants, then I won't say another word about it."

Kylie opened her mouth, but no sound emerged as she was inundated with a maelstrom of conflicting emotions. She fisted her hands tightly at her sides and tried again, "Paul, I—"

"Kylie," Paul cut in gently. "It's not me you should be talking to right now. As you can see, I'm fine now, if rather achy and sleepy. Go take care of what needs to be taken care of. You know where to find me afterwards."

"I'll call the doctor for you, Mr. Moore," Hunter said, wrapping a deliberate arm tightly around Kylie's waist. "I'll also make sure Kylie gets some rest."

Too conflicted to argue, Kylie merely said good-bye to Paul and allowed Hunter to guide her out of the room.

CHAPTER ELEVEN

"I'm curious," Hunter said as he slowly ran a hand soothingly through her hair. "How is it that a Polyshifter can choose which animal to shift into? Do you just think "jaguar" or "tiger" with the desire to shift?"

They were currently lying intertwined on top of the comforter of a bed located in one of the spare rooms on the top floor of the clinic that the hospital provided for the staff. Kylie's head was pillowed on his chest.

She had balked at first when she had walked into the room and had seen the bed—she had been expecting a waiting room or staff break room of some sort—but after some gentle coaxing, she had given in to the desire to be held by him again. She knew she could trust him when he had said that nothing would happen in that room that she didn't one hundred and ten percent want to happen.

Kylie sighed wearily. "I wish it was that easy. Then this whole nightmarish day could have been avoided. No, the trigger is either shifter blood or…" She wrinkled her nose. "…territorial markings. It has to come in contact with my skin. Provided I inherited the right shifter genes, it triggers a change in which animal soul becomes dominant. I was in your territory the night my shifter side was awakened. That's why my first shift was into a jaguar. Unless you have a habit of bleeding all over the place, as embarrassing as it sounds, I must have touched some of your territorial markings when that monster tossed me onto the ground."

"Your hands were once covered with the blood of a human," Hunter pointed out. "Why didn't you revert back into a human?"

"Changing into a pure human is different. Only the saliva of a human can trigger a shift that represses *all* of my animal souls. My father and Paul thought it might be because of a particular enzyme within a human's saliva that negated whatever biological process that allowed us to shift to begin with."

"Polyshifters are more mysterious than I ever imagined," Hunter said.

"We can't all be lion clan spies," Kylie quipped

and then instantly regretted it. What the hell was wrong with her?

Hunter's hand stilled. "You know I feel horrible about immediately thinking that about you, right?" he asked quietly.

"I'm sorry. I shouldn't have said that."

"You're angry," he stated.

"Not at you—at least not anymore. That you rejected me so quickly hurt, yes, but that was mostly my fault. Given what a lot of Polyshifters have done to so many shifter clans on behalf of the lions—well, it would have been stupid for you *not* to be suspicious. I can pretty up my part in the whole mess by saying I was just afraid, that we'd only known each other for a couple days, but while those things are true, it's also true that I *did* deceive you by pretending not to know anything about shifters at all. It was awfully unfair of me to expect any other reaction from you when I wasn't even being completely truthful."

Hunter lifted her chin up with a couple of fingers until her eyes met his. "I don't want you to be angry at yourself, either," he said firmly. "We both could have handled everything a thousand times better, so let's just leave it at that."

He bent his head down and brushed his lips lightly against hers. "Can we start over?"

There were a thousand reasons why she should

get up from that bed and walk away before it was too late. She was bad news. As a Polyshifter, she would always be bad news, a curse to everyone who dared get close to her. Maybe Hunter would hate her for a little while, but that was better than him dying because someone was after *her*.

"I will help you, Kylie," Hunter said gruffly, hugging her body more securely against him. "Maxim, Paul, Karen, and Mitch—we'll all help you. You don't have fight those bastards alone."

To her horror, Kylie felt her eyes begin to well up with tears. It was as though Hunter's words had poked at a ball of hurt she hadn't realized had been festering deep in the bowels of her soul.

She immediately buried her face into his t-shirt. Damned if she would let him see her fall apart.

Hunter tightened his arms around her and rolled them over until his body lay atop hers. Kylie kept her eyes scrunched shut even as she clutched at his shoulders almost desperately. His weight felt good, making her insides start to tingle with warmth and something much more exciting. The urge to cry began to slowly ease as her cheeks began to grow warmer.

He kissed her forehead tenderly, and Kylie's eyes finally opened. His eyes glittered with strength as well as what she imagined was the wild spark of his jaguar soul.

ACCEPTING THE JAGUAR

She slowly opened her legs until Hunter's body naturally settled between them.

"I want you," she admitted.

It was said in a barely audible whisper, but there was no doubt that Hunter's keen jaguar ears heard her loud and clear.

His eyes seemed to flash with an inner light, and then he was devouring her mouth, his tongue thrusting aggressively into her mouth and finding hers ready to join its pleasurable dance.

Kylie's knees tightened around his waist as Hunter began a slow, hard grind against her groin. If he didn't slow down, her panties would be drenched before they even got naked. She tugged at his shirt insistently until he took the hint and pulled himself away from her lips long enough for her to pull it over his head, followed almost immediately by her blouse and bra.

With a mischievous grin, Hunter dipped his head and bit down lightly on one very erect and sensitive nipple, making her involuntarily cry out, before taking it into his mouth and sucking hard. Kylie arched her back and grasped a handful of his hair, tugging at the dark locks in time to his licking and sucking.

Needing something more, she searched blindly for his hand and once found, brought it up to her thus-far-neglected breast. Still guiding his hand, she teasingly slid his fingers slowly over that aching nipple once, then back again before she released him. Hunter slid his thumb over the nub several times, just as slowly, maddeningly as she had shown him, before he abruptly pinched it hard.

"Hunter!"

Kylie bucked her hips and moaned, "Pants off, now! I want to feel your sexy skin sliding against my entire body…"

She only got as far as unbuttoning her jeans before they and her panties were whisked down her legs at the same time faster than she could blink. His own jeans and boxers soon joined hers over the side of the bed.

Then Hunter's body was once again stretched over hers, grinding her down into the mattress as he thrust his hardness against her aching pussy until she moaned.

When his lips once again found hers, Kylie nipped at his bottom lip hard, pleased when a faint, coppery taste flooded her tongue as she licked it. Within moments, Hunter's masculine scent changed to something achingly more familiar and heady.

Hunter pulled away with a gasp. "Kylie you—!" he sputtered, his nostrils flaring several times and the hazel in his eyes becoming more prominent. "You didn't have to do that. It doesn't matter if you're human, a cougar or a jaguar or a bear to me."

"But it does matter," she insisted. "If we do this, if I ultimately decide to stay here in Riverford, then it will be as a jaguar, a member of your clan. What better time to make the change than now?"

Kylie then leaned forward and pressed her nose into his neck and inhaled deeply. "Besides, smelling you like this really turns me on," she said with a wicked grin.

The startled look on Hunter's face quickly turned to something much more lustful. "Then in that case—" He reached down and inserted two of his fingers into her wet passage in one hard thrust, making her squeak and dig her nails into his large, rock-hard biceps. "Let's see if I can't stoke the fires a bit higher."

He hooked his fingers as he began to thrust them in and out, rubbing that spot that never failed to drive her wild while his thumb massaged rough circles over her clit. He then bent down to claim her lips again, swallowing her moans as though he needed them to breathe.

Already on the brink of climax, Kylie reached down to encircle his already leaking cock and gave it a few, aggressive strokes until it was Hunter's turn to moan.

"I want to feel your cock deep inside me," Kylie

pleaded against Hunter's swollen lips.

That delicious fullness pounding into her was something she never thought she would ever feel again, and now that the experience was miraculously within her reach again, she felt as if she would die if she had to wait even just one more minute.

Hunter quickly removed his fingers and positioned himself at her opening. Kylie's breath caught in a split-second of agonizing anticipation before Hunter filled her up to the hilt with a single, powerful thrust. Her muscles clenched around his thick, silky member as she cried out. God, she was already so close, and he hadn't even started to move yet!

Kylie felt her knees being pushed up, opening her up even wider to receive each bone-jarring thrust. Hunter was fucking her like it was the last time, thrusting deeply and more aggressively—dominantly—than he had the previous night. Maybe he really thought it might be. She certainly hadn't been forthcoming on any promises.

But now was certainly not the time to make such an important decision, not when one of the most gorgeous guys on the planet was buried balls deep into her trying his damndest to screw her into the first floor.

Then the pressure building in her groin exploded, and Kylie lost all ability to think at all. She might have screamed, but then her whole world had condensed down to the area between her legs and the pleasurable spasms centered therein. Then a flood of warmth coated her insides, and Hunter groaned into her mouth, thrusting hard and deep a couple more times before collapsing heavily onto her trembling body.

Kylie immediately wrapped her arms around his back and began to kiss every bit of damp skin she could reach on his chest and neck, still caught up in the frenzy her climax had incited. In contrast, Hunter was almost lazily thrusting his still-hard cock shallowly into her as though teasing her, his hips moving in a sort of slow circle.

It wasn't long before she felt his soft lips cover her mouth again, and Hunter spent the next few minutes lovingly kissing her breathless before finally pulling out of her and rolling onto his back, pulling her with him. Kylie laid her head onto his chest and closed her eyes, intent on enjoying the post-climax heaviness in her limbs as well as Hunter's intoxicating scent.

Hunter lightly ran his fingertips along her back, and if Kylie had been a housecat rather than a jaguar, she imagined she would have been purring up a storm.

"So now that you've spilled all your secrets, it's only fair that I return the favor."

Kylie's heart skipped a beat as she raised her head slightly to look up at him. "Why does that sound so ominous?"

His eyes had taken on a solemn tint. "You have good instincts."

She stiffened. "It has something to do with the brother that injured wolf shifter mentioned before he passed out, doesn't it?"

Kylie was ashamed that in all the excitement of the day, she had forgotten completely about him.

Hunter sighed. "And apparently also a good memory. You see, a year ago, Ryder—"

Her phone's ringtone suddenly sounded loudly from somewhere below the bed, making Kylie jump and Hunter curse.

"I'd better get it," she said, reluctantly untangling herself from Hunter's warmth with an apologetic smile. "It might be Karen. I was supposed to call her when dad woke up."

"Oh my God, Kylie, where have you *been*?" her friend, Tara, cried before she could even finish saying hello.

For a split-second, Kylie was thrown a bit off balance. The last person she had been expecting was her friend.

However, before she could rattle off an excuse for her sudden absence, Tara had already started talking again.

"I've been trying to reach you for forever! Kylie,

something terrible has happened to Molly!"

CHAPTER TWELVE

"*Kylie, something terrible has happened to Molly!*"

For a split-second, Kylie stood frozen next to the bed she and Hunter had just made love on, unable to comprehend her friend, Tara's, words as they played over and over within her mind.

"What...?" she whispered almost too low to be heard into her phone.

"What's worse is I haven't been able to get a hold of Ty!" Tara continued frantically as though Kylie hadn't spoken. "We were all supposed to go out for drinks tonight, remember? Molly said you looked like shit last night, so I figured you weren't coming, but when Molly didn't show, either, and didn't call, I went over to her place. There were cops *everywhere*! They told me they think someone broke into her apartment!"

Kylie felt all the blood drain from her face. It couldn't be a coincidence...could it?

"Is she hurt?" she demanded.

Somewhere in some vague corner of her mind, Kylie sensed Hunter abruptly sitting up in the bed behind her.

"That's just it, Kylie!" Tara all but shouted. "I only got a glimpse of her living room because the cops pushed me away before I could get too near Molly's door, but the place was trashed. It looked like a tornado had hit it. The cops wouldn't tell me *anything*, but some of the neighbors were gossiping about there being blood, that they can't find Molly anywhere! I was praying that she and Ty were over at your place! Then you weren't answering your phone and—*Christ*—I thought something had happened to you, too!"

"I haven't seen or talked to Molly since last night when she brought me some meds!" Kylie said, her voice strained with worry. "Where are you right now? Are you alone?"

"I'm still at Molly's apartment complex. The elderly couple that lives next door to her saw me freaking out and invited me to sit down inside their place."

"Good. I'm coming over there right now to pick you up. *Don't* leave that apartment for *any* reason."

"Huh? But the cops want me to go—"

"Especially don't leave with the cops," Kylie added urgently. "I'll explain when I get there."

She tossed the phone on the bed behind her and scrambled after her strewn clothes on the floor. Tara's frantic voice echoed ominously within her mind as

Kylie struggled to pull on her jeans with hands that were shaking with equal panic.

"You know you're doing exactly what they want you to do, right?" Hunter said quietly.

For the first time since she had answered the phone, Kylie glanced over at him. He sat on the edge of the bed, still completely naked, and watched her dress with an unreadable expression.

"I know," Kylie said. She bent over and retrieved his t-shirt from the floor and tossed it to him. "That's why you're going to drive me over there."

He dropped the shirt onto his lap. "Kylie—you know I can't let you step even a foot outside this building right now. We have no idea how many from the lion clan other than that assassin and a handful of Sniffers have managed to infiltrate the city. We have several clansmen on the force. Your friend would be safer leaving that complex in their custody. One phone call from me, and it's done. That'll buy us some time to talk to Maxim. The wolves in his security detail are the best in the city."

Kylie narrowed her eyes angrily at him. "You don't seriously expect me to just hide out here while the lions are out there targeting, *hurting*, my friends?"

Hunter met her gaze calmly. "Yes, I do. Even if I was one hundred percent sure that the lion clans are responsible for what's happened to your friend— which we're *not*—I still wouldn't let you go. Maxim's people have been interrogating the lioness that attacked you and Jack for a few hours now. At the very least we should check in on their progress before we even consider doing anything else. In the meantime, I'll make sure they'll keep your friend safe at the police station until we have a better understanding of the situation, I promise."

Some of the tension in her shoulders eased. "Fine. Hand me my phone, and I'll tell Tara there's been a change of plans while you get dressed."

Instead of reaching for the phone, Hunter stood and reached out both hands to pull her firmly against him into a tight hug. Kylie felt a mild irritation at herself when the subsequent affectionate touch of his lips on her forehead caused a good majority of the rest of her tension to bleed away, and she actually leaned into his embrace. She didn't like to think that she was so weak to crave comfort when so many others had it a thousand times worse right now.

After her parents had disappeared, she had despised having to lean on so many others, and now that she was an adult, it really pissed her off that she found herself *still* needing so many people as much as she did.

"We'll find them," Hunter murmured into her hair, "and we'll make those lion bastards wish they had never stepped foot in our territory."

***

"Hunter, who's Jack?" Kylie asked once Hunter had finished talking to Maxim on the phone.

She was seated on the bed again, trying not to pick a hole in the sheets as she had listened to Hunter's one-sided conversations with first, his contacts within the Riverford PD, and then with Maxim. Hunter had mentioned the name Jack several times during his conversation with his tiger friend.

"That's right…" he replied, coming over to sit down next to her on the bed. "We were interrupted before I could tell you much of anything. Jack's our bleeding wolf friend, a member of the Bray wolf pack and the Parker Grove wolf clan. A lot of the wolves that Maxim employs are from that clan."

"So he survived," Kylie said with a nod of relief. "With those horrible wounds, I really didn't think he would. I couldn't tell from your side of the conversation, but was he one of Maxim's employees?"

Hunter shook his head. "Neither one of us had ever met him, though Maxim knows some of his Bray cousins that live here in this city. No, as I started to tell you before, he knew my older brother, Ryder."

He paused, then reached for one of her hands, taking it into both of his and giving it a firm squeeze. His expression was pinched as though he was trying to contain a surge of sudden emotions, but he couldn't quite keep the brief flash of pain from his eyes.

His smile was bitter. "We share a common wound. Ryder went missing about a year ago."

Kylie gasped sharply, a million questions instantly rising on her tongue, but Hunter was still talking. They would have to wait.

"We were supposed to go for a run in his territory one morning, but when I showed up, he was nowhere to be found. We had always met up in the forest, but I tried his apartment anyway, thinking he might've just slept in. When he didn't answer, I tried calling him. Nothing. He had never blown me off before, so I was worried when a day passed and still no word."

Hunter blew out an angry breath. "It wasn't until he had been missing a month that the Elders took his disappearance a little more seriously. I know I shouldn't be angry about it. Jaguars are known to wander off alone all the time. It's just in our nature, but their utter lack of concern still really pisses me off. However, even I never imagined the horrible truth of what had happened to him."

"The lions," Kylie interjected flatly.

For a split-second, that same look of hatred she had seen in Hunter's eyes when she had confirmed her Polyshifter nature appeared, and her chest tightened painfully with a bout of *déjà vu*. Then the look was gone, replaced with a rage so absolute and searing that it had even her inner jaguar quaking, and a strong urge to *run* washed through her.

"Jack says that they were abducted along with several others, mostly female, and imprisoned in a secret underground facility near Amarillo."

Kylie furrowed her brow. "To use as leverage?"

Hunter's grip on her hand tightened. "No, as guinea pigs."

Her eyes widened. "They were *experimenting* on them? Like—full-on mad scientist experimenting?"

A low growl rose up from his throat as Hunter gave a sharp nod. "I don't know what game those bastards are playing, but from everything Jack told me about the torture they all endured, it's become painfully obvious that the shifter clans opposed against the lion clans really don't know jack shit about the lions' endgame in this silent war."

"But, even taking into account being unexpectedly distracted by me," Kylie said, "the lions have to know that their assassin didn't quite finish the job. For all they know, Jack survived long enough to blab about what they are doing, including their exact location."

She flashed him a stricken look. "You should be concentrating on a rescue rather than bothering with me and my problems! They could be moving all their victims to some other dungeon of horrors!"

"Which is why Maxim and his people are handling all the reconnaissance and preparation rather than me or even the Elders. He has connections all across the state that none of us can ever hope to match. The only thing I can do right now to help my brother is to stay out of Maxim's way and try not to lose myself to my jaguar half that, at the moment, wants to go on a rampage. I need to be as clearheaded and in control as I ever have been in my life for the moment when we can finally make our move."

Hunter released her hand and cupped her face gently with hands that were slightly shaking, betraying just how close to the surface his anger still blazed. "Helping you and your father, helping your friends, is something I *can* do, so there's no reason at all for you to feel guilty. Whether or not your friend, Molly's, disappearance has to do with your run-in with that lioness remains to be seen, but all the same, between the shifters on the force and Maxim's people, if she's still in this city, we'll find her."

Kylie closed her eyes. "I tried to call her boyfriend, Ty, again while you were talking to your contact at the police station, but his phone kept going straight to voicemail," she said. "I'm worried that it isn't just Molly who has disappeared. Tara said that there had been blood found in her apartment. If Ty was there when her apartment was broken into, I don't doubt that he would've tried to protect her with his fists. He's done it before."

"Even so, the blood may not be from any of your friends at all," Hunter pointed out. "Carl told me that the blood found on the scene was minimal. Since this case involves not only a potential kidnapping but also quite possibly those lion bastards, it's been made a high priority among even the humans. We'll know more by the morning."

"I better call Karen and tell her what's what. She and Mitch are hiding out at the house of one of her Elders for the night. If it turns out that Molly *was* targeted because of me, then they may need to keep out of sight for longer than they anticipated."

Hunter caught her wrist as she reached for her phone that was sitting on the bed between them. "Can you please keep what I've told you about the ranch and my brother to yourself for the time being? Right now, the less people that know about it, the better."

"You don't trust them…" Kylie said slowly, her eyes daring him to deny it.

Hunter shook his head. "It's not so much Karen

and Mitch but the people around them. With all the excitement, I never did get around to telling you this, but a few days ago, I found evidence that a Polyshifter may have entered the city. Given that the most recent suspected Sniffers are cougars…"

Kylie felt her heart seize painfully. "It's a wonder that you didn't go for my throat the second you realized what I was."

"That's why I said I was dangerous. I *should* have taken you down instantly, but I *couldn't*. Had you truly been a spy for the lions, I could've jeopardized *everything* because I let my emotions drown out any semblance of reason."

"I'm sorry," she said, hanging her head in guilt.

He leaned forward and pressed his forehead against hers. "You and I can apologize to each other until we're both blue in the face, but it won't change how fucked up things are right now. We both fucked up; let's just leave it at that. All we can do now is lie in the bed we've made and hope that everything turns out okay in the end."

CHAPTER THIRTEEN

A sudden knock on the door had both of them stiffening.

Hunter immediately raised his nose to scent the air and then almost in the same instant, his shoulders relaxed.

"It's Maxim," he said with obvious relief as he rose to let the tiger shifter into the room.

"Who did you think it was?" Kylie asked suspiciously.

He flashed her a wry grin. "Gaither, but that's a discussion better left for another time."

"Or not at all," Kylie muttered under her breath as Maxim entered the room—and then promptly walked back out.

"Can we talk somewhere a little less—aromatic?"

Maxim called from the hall with obvious amusement, eliciting a grin from Hunter.

Frowning at both men, Kylie joined Hunter at the door without a word. Now really wasn't the time to joke, but she still allowed him to thread their hands together without even a token fuss. Truth be told, the warmth of his hand kept the panic that was still simmering at the surface of her emotions at bay. It reminded her that she and Paul weren't alone this time, that there were powerful people that were able and willing to help them.

Hunter led them into another empty room at the end of the hall identical to the one they had just left. She and Hunter sat on the bed while Maxim pulled up a chair and sat facing them. Seeing the tiger shifter up close, Kylie couldn't help but notice just how tired and ragged he looked from his eyes alone, as though he hadn't slept in days.

She could feel her entire body tense in response. Just what bad news was he about to bring them that would have him looking so beaten down?

For his part, Maxim was looking at their joined hands in something like bemusement. However, when he realized that she was staring at him, he flashed her a small smile, and his posture showed a bit more life.

"It's really good to see that you two have worked everything out," Maxim said. "We'll all need you both at your best during the next few days."

Hunter eagerly leaned forward. "You've found it."

Maxim nodded. "From what I've been able to

find out, the ranch Jack Bray described is owned by a human Silicon Valley tech billionaire—at least on paper. It operates as a legit cattle ranch that's been turning a hefty profit for over two decades. It's no wonder it's never fallen under suspicion until now. Their invasion into this state runs a helluva lot deeper than any of us ever imagined."

"And the assassin?" Hunter asked. "Have you managed to get anything out of her?"

"Not a peep. My men were still working on her when I left, but she'll probably turn out to be a dead end. I've heard all my life that no one from a lion clan, even a Rogue, has ever betrayed their secrets, and I seriously doubt this one will be the first."

"My friend, Karen, told me that shifter criminals are rarely sent to the same prisons as humans but dealt with by the individual clans," Kylie interjected. "I imagine a lion prisoner would be treated differently as it affects all clans, really, no matter that it was just my family and friends and Jack Bray that she attacked in this instance."

"Do we kill our lion prisoners, you mean?" Maxim replied bluntly.

Kylie blinked at him in surprise. "Not at all. The only things about the inner workings of a shifter clan I know are from what Karen and Mitch have been willing to tell me and the little I've experienced at Hunter's side. I just wanted to know how these things are usually handled among shifters. For the sake of my real parents, there are things, questions that I'd want asked now that you have an actual lion in custody. I'm just wondering if that would be possible?"

Maxim's eyes softened. "Understandable."

"There's still a lot I don't know about shifter society, you know," she admitted. "I've lived my whole life as a human. Their rules are the only ones I've known. Hell, I'm not even sure what you two plan to do about my secret, where I'll stand within Riverford's shifter society once this whole mess plays out." She turned to Hunter. "You did seem to expect a visit from Mr. Gaither earlier."

Hunter made a face as though he had swallowed a whole lemon. "Whom we will *not* be telling that you're a Polyshifter if we can at all help it. I think we can all agree on at least that much. With all these Sniffers and assassins suddenly prowling around the city pretty much right under our noses for God-only-knows how long, I don't need to be a psychic to tell you what'll happen. For now, the Elders are content enough with me keeping an eye on you here."

"As for the ranch," Maxim said, "I have several people keeping an eye out for any suspicious movement as well as devising a plan of attack. I'm afraid there's not much else we can do tonight but wait for my people to report back to me in the morning."

"How long do you think we have, max, before they move all the abductees as a precaution?" Hunter asked. "Because I don't doubt for a second that the clan that sent that lioness here doesn't know their little assassin's been captured, that she's failed."

"Word is being spread throughout both the Riverford and Parker Grove communities that Jack Bray is currently in a coma and hidden away in a private facility. That may delay them for the few days we'll need to organize a rescue."

"As well as invite a whole slew of those bastards like iron fillings to a magnet," Hunter added dryly. He glanced at Kylie worriedly. "With a 'Rogue lion' and an informant—both with the very real potential of bringing down their entire operations in this state—within the same area, it may very well give them the excuse to come at us openly and at full-force. Dangling Jack like that may come back to bite us in the ass hard."

"We'll just have to make sure we rescue all of them before the shit hits the fan, won't we?" Maxim suddenly fixed her with a serious look. "Which brings us to our last problem."

Kylie stiffened. "If you expect me to leave the city while Paul's bedbound and my friend's still missing—" she began hotly.

"I don't," Maxim cut in mid-rant, "though your friend, Molly, *is* what I wanted to talk to you about."

This time it was Kylie's turn to anxiously lean forward. "Do you know what happened to her?" she demanded.

"Yes and no," he replied maddeningly. "After a few shifters from the department arrived at your friend's apartment at Hunter's request, they of course knew immediately that a shifter had recently been in that unit—and it wasn't a jaguar."

"I haven't been to her place since my shifter side awakened," Kylie confirmed. "Was it—was it a lion?"

Hunter squeezed her hand in comfort, but Maxim was shaking his head. "An alligator, of all things. If it's one thing we ever agreed on with the gator clan, it was our mutual hatred of the lions, so I'm hesitant to believe that the gator in question was a local."

"...or if it even *was* a *gator* shifter at all," Hunter added, looking at Kylie pointedly.

For a split-second Kylie stared back at him blankly before she gasped in sudden understanding.

A Polyshifter.

"So," Hunter continued, "either the fact that your friend had an apparent violent run-in with a shifter only hours after you, yourself, were attacked as a Rogue is the biggest coincidence in the world, or the lions really have managed to sneak in the very weapon all clans opposed to them fear the most. If so, that they're choosing to use their best hand now in what I can only guess is to force Kylie to come forward in order to silence her opens up a whole new can of worms."

"Which means bringing down whatever the hell it is they're doing at that 'ranch' in the Panhandle just got a whole lot more important than just us wanting to rescue Anna and Ryder," Maxim said grimly. "After I was done here, I was going to go have another chat with my Elders about organizing an emergency assembly of all the Riverford clan Elders tomorrow morning. Now..."

"Yes, now..." Hunter echoed, his eyes double pools of equal worry and frustration.

Kylie looked between them. "Do you think knowing that a Polyshifter is likely mixed up in this whole mess will make them more reluctant to help you get your brother back?" she asked, unable to understand this sudden strange mood between them.

"No, that at least one of the Elders will be *too* interested," Hunter said, his voice suddenly deadly serious.

Kylie stilled completely as the horror of his words sunk in. "Could they have infiltrated that far up in a clan's hierarchy?" she asked quietly.

"The lion clans are said to have the patience of immortals," Maxim answered. "It's pretty much common knowledge that it was the method used to take control of the clans in both Philadelphia and Chicago."

"With just *one* Polyshifter?" Kylie exclaimed in disbelief.

She sagged a bit in relief when the tiger shook his head. That a person, even someone as extraordinary as a Polyshifter, could have that much power was too frightening to even contemplate.

"While no one is sure about the exact number," he replied, "most agree that it was at least a dozen, weaseling their way into several different clans over the span of around fifty to sixty years. The lions never have done anything half-assed."

"The evidence I found the other day was too vague to tell us much of anything," Hunter cut in. "At this point, suspecting one of the Elders of being a Polyshifter or even the alligator that allegedly kidnapped your friend is just that—speculation. We just don't have enough intel. If that damned assassin would only—"

Her eyes widening, Kylie abruptly tore her hand out of Hunter's and all but lunged at a startled Maxim, grabbing his forearms tightly in rising panic. "Please tell me that none of your Elders have had access to the lioness assassin!" she said urgently.

"Kylie, what—" Hunter began in bewilderment, but she cut him off.

"They'll *know*, Hunter!" she cried, letting go of Maxim and turning her attention to Hunter again. "Don't you see? That lioness had to have had plenty of time to meet with any spies, whether Sniffers or Polyshifters, in the city between attacking us in the forest and then attacking me at Karen's, but she *still didn't know that I was a Polyshifter.* Whoever the Polyshifter is masquerading as, Elder or just a normal clansman/woman, every shifter in this city's at least heard of the new jaguar Returner. You said so, yourself."

Hunter nodded hesitantly, and Kylie drew in a deep breath in order to calm her racing heart before she continued, "It should have been a given that the lioness would've found out that the Rogue lioness she had been hunting and the jaguar Returner were one and the same, but unless that assassin is one hell of an actress, she honestly thought I was a Rogue back at Karen's. Maybe she wanted the glory or satisfaction of capturing me all by herself, I don't know, but for whatever reason, that assassin must not have talked with any of her allies within the city. Her ignorance about my true heritage doesn't make any sense otherwise."

"She does have a point," Maxim said. "I don't think that lioness would've gone after Kylie alone had she known she would be dealing with a Polyshifter not under their control. Regardless, you don't have anything to worry about, Kylie. Yes, my Elders know that I have a captured lioness on my hands. However, only Lana, myself, and the head of my security even know where I'm holding her, and I plan on keeping it that way for now.

"You also don't have to worry about any of them infiltrating any of the wolf clans. A wolf shifter's nose is leagues better than any other shifter species, so the lions have always steered clear of them during their campaigns. As long as you play the jaguar as you are now and don't have any more slipups, then your secret should be safe."

Kylie pinched the bridge of her nose, feeling a tension headache coming on. "I'll keep that in mind," she replied dryly.

An unfamiliar ringtone suddenly filled the air, causing Kylie to jump. Hunter ran a hand soothingly down her back as Maxim dug his phone out of his overcoat. He glanced down at the screen before lifting it to his ear. "Yes?"

He listened stoically for what felt like an eternity before ending the call with a parting, "I'll be right there."

Maxim stood up. "It seems something interesting regarding one of the suspected Sniffers my people have been tailing has come to light. One of my wolves

has a video that I need to review ASAP. In the meantime, call Jack Bray and see what the Parker Grove
clans can offer in forms of aid. I don't think it should
wait until morning."

"Agreed," Hunter said.

At the door, Maxim paused with his hand on the
knob. "Anna and Ryder *will* be coming home soon,"
he growled, turning back to look at them with barely
contained anger.

"Anna?" Kylie vaguely remembered Hunter mentioning that name before.

"You didn't tell her?" Maxim asked, mild surprise
bleeding into the inferno within his eyes.

Hunter shook his head. "I didn't think it was my
place."

The smile that stretched his lips was incredibly sad
and full of pain. "Anna Barkova. My mate-to-be. She
went missing six months ago."

Kylie's heart sank in horror. "She's—that
ranch—"

The renewed rage in Maxim's blue eyes was all the
answer she needed.

CHAPTER FOURTEEN

"You're crazy if you think I'll be able to get any sleep after all of that," Kylie grumbled, but she still allowed Hunter to pull her into his arms after he had propped himself up against the headboard with a couple of pillows.

"At least try," Hunter coaxed as she settled against him, her head on his chest. "Who knows when you'll get another chance. Negotiations between clans, especially the clans of different cities are tedious at the best of times. I'll probably be on the phone for hours, not to mention that I *did* promise your dad that I'd make sure you got some rest."

Kylie blew out a frustrated breath. "My friend, Molly's, missing, maybe even hurt. Probably because of me. I should at least be down with Tara at the police station. It just doesn't seem right that you and Maxim are doing all of the work while I sleep the night away. There must be *something* I can do to help."

Hunter hugged her more tightly against him. "You have no idea how much you *are* helping me by just being here with me, and I'm not saying that lightly. You may not see it, but I'm barely keeping a reign on my jaguar. The human part of me knows that the best chance my brother, Anna, and all those other captive shifters have is to gather as much information as possible and plan our next move carefully, but my jaguar half just wants to race over to that ranch and start tearing out throats. Without you here to remind myself of the costs, I doubt even Maxim would've been able to talk sense into me after a while."

Kylie pressed her nose against his chest and inhaled deeply. Until that moment, she had never considered that anger had a scent, but—*something* was definitely strongly present among the scents she had come to associate with Hunter that she had never smelled before. Neither metallic nor earthy or even acrid, it was a scent that was more a sensation than having any sort of distinguishable fragrance.

She glanced at the door, wondering if Maxim had given off a similar scent. She had been too distracted by the revelation about Anna to pay attention to the scents swirling around in the air. How much more information was she missing because she was still too new to the animal side of her shifter nature?

A light tug on her hair had Kylie looking up at Hunter's face. "What is it?" he asked.

"I had no idea that your reason was that close to snapping, and that really bothers me," she admitted.

"Even filled with rage, I would never hurt you if that's what you're worried about."

Kylie shook her head. "That's not what I mean. I just realized that I might as well have been blind because I'm still not used to living as a shifter. If I would have bothered to pay attention to the scents coming off you, I would've known something was up with both you and Maxim even if I hadn't known exactly what that new scent meant. I guess what I'm trying to say is I've suddenly realized exactly how vulnerable I've been since the shifter part of me awakened, and now I'm worried about what else I might have missed that my jaguar senses had been screaming at me. What if that lioness had been watching from the forest when Paul picked me up from your apartment complex this morning? It didn't even occur to me to pay attention to the scents around me! What if that was the reason she was able to find us at Karen's? She saw Paul's license plate, used it to find out his name and from there, my name. What if I'm wrong and the lioness *did* report me as a Rogue to someone in her clan before she went after me, to one of their Polyshifter allies? Then when Maxim's people took her prisoner, the Polyshifter decided to go with Plan B and kidnap Molly in order to get to me—"

"That's a lot of 'what ifs,'" Hunter cut her off firmly before Kylie could work herself up even more. "We still don't know for sure if the lions are involved with her disappearance, and even if they are, if that alligator shifter the cops smelled in your friend's apartment really *is* a Polyshifter. At this point, it's all pure speculation, and God knows *I* tormented myself on all the 'what ifs' and 'maybes' after Ryder went missing." He ran his free hand affectionately through her hair. "I would save you from that agony if I can."

Kylie flashed him a guilty look. "You're right. This isn't the time to be freaking out about stuff like that, especially when I'm keeping you from calling Jack."

"And keeping yourself from resting," he scolded teasingly.

"I'll close my eyes, but that's all I can promise."

Hunter wasn't on the phone longer than five minutes before a slight tensing of his body had Kylie opening her eyes and looking up at him questionably. She hadn't heard anything on his end that would have warranted his sudden tension.

"I'll be there in twenty."

The wary look in his eyes had her instantly on red alert. Kylie pulled away and rose to her knees beside him before he could speak to her.

"Don't even think about it," she warned.

"Kylie…"

"You're not leaving me behind here," she said mulishly, "especially if you're going to see Jack."

"I am, but where I need to go is clear across town," he said. "It's not safe for you to be seen. You know that. Maybe not even for a few days."

Kylie blinked in surprise. "Across town? I thought you said his family was taking him back to

Parker Grove."

Hunter studied her face for a long, tense moment before he sighed in something like resignation and replied, "I thought so, too, but it seems his family felt he would be safer recovering somewhere other than a hospital or even the family home. A few Elders from both the Riverford and Parker Grove wolf clans are with him right now, and they want to talk face-to-face. I'm not sure they would appreciate me bringing extra people, particularly someone as high-profile as you."

Her shoulders sagged. Damn, but she couldn't really argue with that. "Fine. You win."

Hunter grinned before leaning over to give her a firm kiss. "I know sitting around sucks, but I really do think it's best that you stay here tonight. Just be sure to lock the door behind me, and don't open it to anyone other than me or Maxim."

She nodded. "As long as you're going out, can you do something for me?"

"Maxim's people already brought you and your father's bags from Karen's house if that's what you're asking," Hunter said. "They're in the room we just left. I can—"

"That wasn't what I was going to ask, but that's good to know," Kylie interjected. "I'd like you to pick up a different bag, the one I left wrapped in a trash bag in your guestroom's closet."

He looked at her sharply. "You mean the one swimming in your 'come fuck me now' pheromones? Why in the world would you even want me to go near it?"

Kylie smiled at him sheepishly. "Because of what I hid inside. Given the deep shit I'm in right now, I think it would be dangerous not to have it from now on."

Hunter frowned. "A gun?" he guessed.

"A good idea probably, but no. It's a br—"

Three successive sharp knocks on the door had both of them freezing, before Hunter barked out as he scrambled off the bed, "Yes?"

"Oh, good, you're here," Donald Gaither's unmistakable voice called through the door a split-second before it opened.

Kylie felt a brief moment of relief that they were both fully clothed except for their shoes and Hunter was off the bed. Neither one had thought to lock the door after Maxim had left. She did her best to school her expression to something polite and benign as the Elder's gaze swept the room before landing squarely on her. The last thing they needed was this man to catch wind of their relationship.

"Hello again, Kylie," Gaither said. "I was hoping we could speak for a moment."

"Hello," she replied, trying her best to sound friendly and at the same time not to fidget under his unblinking gaze.

"Not now, Gaither," Hunter said shortly as he bent to gather Kylie's sneakers from the floor. "We were just on our way out to go pick up some of Kylie's father's things from his house before it gets too late. I think we can both agree that it would be best that they both stay here for at least the next few days."

Thinking it best to let him do the talking, Kylie accepted her shoes without a word and began putting them on. She had to struggle to keep from smirking as she watched the two men. It was starting to look as though she wouldn't have to stay behind after all.

"There's no need for both of you to go," Gaither insisted. "I can stay here with Kylie. It'll give us a chance to talk about a few things."

Yeah—she *really* didn't want to be alone with this man given the grilling she had endured the last time she had seen him.

Thinking fast, Kylie said, "Um—sorry but my father's security system needs a thumbprint to deactivate, so I *have* to go."

"Then I'm afraid I'll have to insist on you going in the morning," Gaither said, "maybe when more of us can accompany you. For now, I'd like you both to accompany me to one of the conference rooms where a few of the other Elders of our clan are waiting. As this is the first instance in a long time that we have definitive proof of a lion actually infiltrating the city and attacking one of our own, there is much we need to discuss."

"I will, but *after* I go to my father's house," Kylie replied stubbornly just as Hunter opened his mouth to probably protest again. "There's something I'd like to retrieve, something private that he needs."

The older man frowned. "I'm afraid I must insist—"

"Insist all you want, but we're going," Hunter growled as he took one of Kylie's hands and pulled her to her feet. "Things are fucked up enough in her life without you trying to manhandle her into a conversation that she obviously doesn't want to have at the moment. After what she's been through in the last couple of days, the least you can do is allow her a little peace of mind before she has to jump back into all the muck."

As Hunter tugged her past the Elder, Kylie saw Gaither's nostrils flare and his eyes narrow. She closed her eyes and groaned mentally, wondering what exactly he was smelling on her—pheromones or Hunter, himself. So much for keeping just how far they had progressed in their relationship a secret.

CHAPTER FIFTEEN

"S ince it seems I'll be going with you after all," Kylie said as Hunter continued to tug her down the hall towards the elevators in a brisk walk, "we might need to stop in the room where you stashed my bags. I can grab a hoodie and somewhat disguise myself."

He glanced back at her with a disgruntled frown. "I suppose it won't hurt."

"I know you're mad, but Mr. Gaither interrupting and forcing the issue might be for the best considering what I was about to ask you to retrieve for me."

They were stopped at the door to the room where they had made love earlier. Hunter glance worriedly both ways, but there was still no sign of the Elder. He hurried her inside and locked the door behind them.

"Keep your voice down," he warned. "I don't

doubt that Gaither is literally sniffing around the room we just left wondering what we're really up to besides the obvious, but he'll be coming this way soon. I would rather he not hear any of our conversations."

Kylie nodded grimly. "You're worried he might be the Polyshifter."

Hunter surprisingly shook his head. "Maxim brought up the very good point that Gaither's too blatantly nosy to fit the profile, but that also means he has the best chance out of all our Elders to come in frequent contact with an actual spy from the lion clans. Although he can help us quite a bit, I would rather he not know too much about what we just discussed with Maxim until we can figure out whether or not there's actually another Polyshifter in Riverford other than you." He pointed to a pile of familiar duffle bags next to a small dresser. "Now, grab your hoodie and let's get going. Maybe we can still beat Gaither out of here."

"Do we have time to stop at your apartment before we head over to see Jack?" she asked as she riffled through one of the bags.

"Is what you wanted me to get for you that important?"

She stood with the aforementioned black hoodie and slipped it on over her head. "Definitely. Now more so than ever. It's a charm bracelet that belonged to my mother."

"A bracelet?" Hunter echoed confusedly.

"It looks pretty innocuous, but the hollowed-out insides of the oval charms are coated with the blood of various shifters."

His eyes widened in sudden understanding. "Now I see why you hid it from me, but why bring it near me at all at the time?"

"Because it was one of the things that saved me from the torture of jaguar heat," Kylie replied dryly. "The heat was literally driving me crazy, so it was either call you and beg for you to come back and screw me—something neither of us were really ready for at that point—or take a chance with turning myself completely human again. I figured I could use the fact that no one knew very much about Returners as an excuse about the heat miraculously disappearing. Before Jennifer arrived, Paul sent over one of his toothbrushes and the bracelet with Molly. I managed to get rid of the heat and reawaken my jaguar soul with no one being the wiser."

Hunter's expression suddenly hardened. "Jennifer met Molly?"

Kylie grabbed onto his arm. "Wait! You don't think…!"

"I don't think we can rule anything out at this point," he said. "I'll talk to Maxim about getting some of his people to watch the Grahams."

He reached over and lifted her hood over her head. "Come on," he said, threading their hands together and tenderly kissing her lips briefly. "We'll pick up your bracelet before heading over to meet Jack and his Elders."

***

137

The poor excuse for a building that loomed ahead was the last place Kylie would have expected anyone to be taken to unless they planned on putting a couple of bullets into the back of their head. Located in one of the older industrial areas on the north side of the city, the corroded sheet metal and steel building looked to have been a warehouse for farming equipment sometime during the dawn of time.

"Are we meeting Elders or Mafiosi?" Kylie quipped with a nervous laugh. "This isn't exactly the kind of place I imagined a clan of wolves would gather."

"Which was their intention, I'm sure," Hunter replied with a grin as he shut off his headlights and drove around to the back of the large building.

He parked behind a couple of large, broken-down tractors that were slowly being taken over by an assortment of tall weeds and saplings.

"It doesn't look like anyone's even here," Kylie said, eying the darkened warehouse warily.

"I suspect someone'll be out shortly to escort us in," Hunter said.

"Good, because it looks like the kind of place where stepping on a rusty nail and getting tetanus would be the least of your worries."

A loud knock abruptly sounded against her window, and Kylie nearly jumped clear out of her skin. A dark-haired man around thirty stood just outside her door, bending down to peer inside.

Hunter reached over and gave her shoulder a

comforting squeeze. "Don't worry. That's just Adam, a wolf shifter from the Bray pack."

"Last week if someone would've told me that I would be sneaking around a creepy, abandoned warehouse with a hot guy in order to have a secret meeting with a pack of what are essentially werewolves after being attacked by a werelion, I would've thought they were more than crazy," Kylie grumbled. "It's almost too absurd to be believed."

At least Adam looked somewhat contrite as he shook her hand after Hunter introduced them.

"My cousin's glad that you've come as well," Adam said to her as he led them to a partially-opened door in the left corner of the warehouse. "He wanted to thank you in person."

"I'm glad I could come, too," Kylie replied. "Considering how awful he looked when I last saw him, I wanted to see how he was doing, but—are you sure your Elders are okay with me being here?"

From what she had heard of their phone conversation when Hunter had called Jack again after retrieving her mom's bracelet to explain why he was suddenly bringing her along, the long pauses between exchanges of words likely signified their hesitation, if not Jack's, then with his Elders.

Adam snorted. "Are you kidding? They've been dying to meet the jaguar clan's new Returner since word first spread about you. They'll never admit it, of course, and I imagine they'll have a few questions for you."

"Of course they will," Hunter said wryly as he

wrapped a comforting arm around Kylie's waist, probably sensing her dismay.

Inside, it was just as dark and creepy as she had imagined. Pieces of old farming equipment covered with enough cobwebs to house an entire city of spiders lined the walls and were also scattered haphazardly throughout the entire interior. She found herself sneezing almost uncontrollably as what seemed like a thousand years of dust and a multitude of smells assaulted her senses. Old motor oil, possibly rust, and pesticides were among the most potent, the strength of them more so than she would have thought given the air of abandonment. She wondered if they had been added on purpose as she couldn't even smell a hint of wolf among that acrid combination of stink.

They followed Adam along a narrow path between the warehouse walls and the old equipment and stopped when they had reached nearly half its length. The wolf then squatted down and pulled on a handle of a trapdoor in the concrete floor. Even with her slightly enhanced night vision, Kylie could barely make out the outline of a few stone steps leading down into the darkness.

Kylie pulled out her cell phone, and clutched it tightly. There was no way she was going down what was essentially a hole in the ground without at least the promise of light literally within the palm of her hand.

She nearly hissed when Adam suddenly released a series of loud growls into the gloom instead of descending. An answering howl immediately followed from below and some of her tension eased.

Must have been the secret word to get in, Kylie thought, pressing her lips together firmly in order to staunch an absurd need to giggle as Hunter gently ushered her towards the steps after Adam.

She paused a few steps down in order to wait for Hunter. She couldn't help but feel claustrophobic once he pulled the trapdoor closed behind him, plunging them into near absolute darkness. Kylie started to feel for the "on" button at the top of her phone, but then the stairway abruptly flooded with light, making her scrunch her eyes closed with a startled cry.

"Sorry about that," she heard Adam say sheepishly as Hunter cursed.

Kylie cautiously opened her eyes and blinked them rapidly as they slowly adjusted. She was finally able to see that the stairs went down pretty deep.

"Wow, does this lead to the Batcave or something?" she asked with a laugh.

Adam turned around and grinned. "I wish it was that awesome. It looks more like a secret military bunker from World War II. Probably built around that time, come to think of it."

At the bottom, Adam led them down a long tunnel to a thick iron door at the end that was flanked by a couple of men.

"Good. The old bastards were getting antsy," the blond man on the left said. He then flashed Kylie a curious look before he focused his attention on Hunter. "It's been a while, Hunter."

"Yeah. Sorry it had to be under these circumstances," Hunter replied. He nodded towards Kylie.

"This is Kylie Moore, our clan's newest addition and my—partner."

Kylie was a bit startled at the introduction, but she schooled her expression into a friendly smile as she reached out to shake the hands of the two wolf guards. "It's nice to meet you."

The iron door opened with a screech that put her in mind of a medieval dungeon. She shuddered, hoping the room beyond would be a bit more spacious. If not, it was going to be a long night.

CHAPTER SIXTEEN

*K*ylie breathed an audible sigh of relief as they stepped into what looked like a large community room filled with comfortable-looking couches and chairs. There was even a large flat-screen mounted on one of the natural rock walls, though it was currently off. However, the room, itself, was empty of people.

Adam gestured towards one of the smaller couches. "Make yourselves comfortable, and I'll go let the Elders and Jack know you're here."

Once they were settled and Adam had disappeared into a door across the room, Kylie turned to Hunter and said with a frown, "This is kinda unnerving, you know. If I had known that we would be taken underground, I might not have been so insistent in tagging along. I'm *really* claustrophobic."

Hunter snaked his arm around her waist again and gave her a gentle squeeze. "Just imagine that we're meeting in a back room at Maxim's club if things start to feel a little tight."

"And to think that you made fun of me when I thought you were totally serious about meeting your Elders in a cave," she scolded.

He chuckled. "In my defense, I've never been down here. Most clans are pretty tight-lipped about their—safe houses, I suppose. That we were allowed down here at all shows how dire the situation really is."

Before Kylie could reply, the door Adam had exited the room through swung open, and a group of ten, solemn-faced men and women filed in. Both Kylie and Hunter stood up to greet them.

Introductions were made all around and then everyone finally settled down onto the couches with the two jaguars as the focal point.

"Adam will be here shortly with Jack and his father," Glen, one of the oldest men in the bunch said. "Although Jack is far from recovered, he insisted on being present for at least a portion of our discussion."

Hunter nodded. "Whatever is most comfortable for him."

"Although many from our clan work for the Siberian, Maxim Clarke, we also sent out our own small reconnaissance team earlier in the day to the Panhandle. They are currently staking out the various roads surrounding the lions' ranch as well as the ranch, itself. We can only hope something useful will present itself within the next few hours, but at the very least, if they try to move their captives offsite, we'll be in a better position to follow."

"Any luck on getting that lioness to talk?" one of the women asked.

"Don't hold your breath," Hunter warned. "We've found and removed one threat out of many. That's the best we can hope from one of the bastards' assassins."

"And the alleged Sniffers?" another asked.

"Maxim's people may have more on that shortly, but it's beginning to look like the lions have managed to slip more of their people into the city than we thought." He glanced over at the three Elders from the Parker Grove clan, and added, "You might want to spread the word to the other clans of your city to keep a sharper eye on all visiting shifters. I don't know why, but it seems the lions are getting a hell of a lot bolder."

Glen nodded. "I've already contacted our clansmen that work security and surveillance in various places throughout the city to do the same."

"You should also keep an eye on the alligator clan," Hunter said, causing Kylie to stiffen in surprise. She hadn't thought that Hunter would bring up anything to do with what had happened to Molly. "At least one may be tied to all the brouhaha caused by that lioness in the last twenty-four hours, but we're not sure if the gator in question is an outsider. Once we learn more, either Maxim or I'll pass on the info."

Some of the Elders began quietly murmuring in troubled tones, but before anyone else could speak, the door at the back of the room opened, and Adam entered, followed by a heavily bandaged and pale Jack being pushed in a wheelchair by an older man whom Kylie presumed was his father. The poor wolf shifter was barely managing to sit upright, hollow-eyed and still looking seconds away from collapsing. Given what Hunter had told her about Jack's mate also being one of those still being held captive, his appearance nor his insistence in being included despite the severity of his injuries wasn't all that shocking.

Kylie rose, wanting to greet him face-to-face. Her sudden movement instantly caught Jack's eye, and he lifted his head to blearily peer back at her. Then without warning, Jack jerked forward so violently that he nearly fell out of the wheelchair had Adam not reached out with lightning-fast reflexes to catch him with a startled curse.

"*You*!" Jack cried, his eyes wide and wild as he stared back at her as though she was a ghost.

Instinctually, Kylie took a step back, bumping into Hunter's front as he was suddenly standing behind her. She felt his arms wrap firmly, protectively, around her waist as she looked back at Jack in sudden fear.

Shit! Did he see me shift into a lion after all?

"*How* in the hell did you escape?" Jack demanded roughly, his voice cracking at the end. Then more desperately, "Did you see my mate, Maya? A red wolf? Is she okay?"

"What are you—" Kylie began in bewilderment, but then Jack started wheezing harshly as though he had been hit with a sudden, brutal asthma attack.

Hunter pulled her farther back, his body taunt with tension. "Maybe he's flashing back to his captivity," he said hesitantly. "I should probably take Kylie out into the passageway—"

"I'm *not* flashing back!" Jack yelled. He was now standing and struggling to break out of his father's hold. He pointed a finger at her. "You were *there*! I saw them dragging you down the halls lots of times! One of the cougars!"

No one said a word as they all looked from Jack to her with varying expressions from confusion to the worst, suspicion. Jack's father looked stricken.

"Jack," Hunter said in a soft, soothing voice, "this is Kylie Moore. She's the *jaguar* that was with me in the woods when you stumbled onto us. Just take a moment and sniff her. You'll see."

Kylie looked over her shoulder and said, "Let me go to him so he can see me properly."

He nodded and released her only to take her hand. She didn't think the distraught man would attack her, but she didn't say anything and tugged Hunter along with her until she stood only a foot away from the wolf shifter.

Jack stared at her for a long, uncomfortable moment before he slowly leaned towards her and visibly sniffed her as suggested. The wild look in his eyes was instantly replaced with utter confusion.

"Jaguar," he said finally after staring at her hard for what felt like a small eternity. "Even though it's a little strange, you definitely smell like a jaguar."

"She's a Returner," Hunter said quickly. "Her scent's always been a little different since her first shift."

He was probably thinking the same thing she was, that letting a *wolf shifter* get a good whiff of her wasn't the best idea. Jack was likely picking up the faint, underlying scent of her Polyshifter heritage.

Jack nodded slowly, and all his earlier energy

seemed to drain out of him all at once. He sagged in his father's arms with a grimace of pain, and the older man immediately lowered him back down into the wheelchair.

"Sorry," Jack said wearily. "My sight was fading, so I didn't get a good look at you before I passed out in the forest. I'm sorry if I scared you. It's just—your hair, your face—you look just like one of the cougars being held prisoner in that pit of hell, and I hoped..."

His face crumbled, unable to say the rest.

A thus far silent Adam reached over and put a comforting hand on Jack's shoulder. "We'll get Maya out," he said, dark eyes flashing with fierce determination. He looked back at Hunter. "We'll get them *all* out."

Jack raised a hand weakly to clasp Adam's forearm in a show of gratitude before he turned his gaze to the group of Elders. "I heard them call that cougar 'Grace,'" he said. "We should ask the cougar clan's Elders if anyone by that name has gone missing within the last few years."

A large chasm suddenly opened up in the pit of Kylie's stomach and swallowed her whole. It had to be a coincidence. It had to...but...!

Mom...

CHAPTER SEVENTEEN

"Are you okay?" Kylie heard Adam ask, his voice sounding muffled and distant as though the length of a football field separated them, but she couldn't drag her mind away from the horrible conclusion that her thoughts had reached enough to answer him.

A cougar. Her name was Grace. Could it be?

Suddenly, Hunter was standing in front of her and tilting her chin up with a firm grip. "Kylie, what's wrong?" he demanded, his eyes swimming with worry.

"I-I need to—need to leave," she stuttered, shaking her head a little until she could focus on his face. She grabbed Hunter's arms and squeezed them urgently. "I need to check with—Hunter, I think I might *know* her! Grace, I mean."

Several people gasped as Kylie fixed Hunter with anguished eyes, willing him to understand what she was trying to tell him. She couldn't say it, not in front of these people.

"We need to talk to *Paul!*" she insisted, willing him to get what she was insinuating.

She knew the moment he understood, though his eyes only widened a fraction, but Kylie had seen it, the horror that had also flashed fleetingly within his eyes.

Hunter looked over at the Elders and said, "If she's right… Either way, I need to take her to speak with the cougar clan Elders right now. Sorry to run out on you so abruptly, especially when it was me that requested this meeting, but I'll be back as soon as I can to resume our discussions. Maybe by then, Maxim'll have more info for us, or maybe even be able to join us."

"Go. We'll be down here all night, so take all the time you need," Glen said. "I'll have Jack text you my number. Call, and we'll send Adam out to meet you again when you return."

Within minutes they were back on the surface and hurrying through the weeds to Hunter's truck. Only when they were inside did Kylie lose her grip on the thundering emotions that she had been struggling to keep from breaking loose. Her face scrunched up, and silent tears began to fall at the thought that her mother may very well still be alive, that after over a decade of looking, she may have finally found her in the worst place imaginable.

Hunter just as quietly reached over and enveloped her within his arms. She melted into his warmth and closed her eyes, her breath hitching as she cried softly.

"After my parents had been missing for two years," she said thickly against his neck, "I knew deep down that they were dead, that what Paul, Laura, and I were really looking for was the 'how' and not them at all. Then to suddenly find out that she might be in that horrible place being *t-tortured*...experimented on..."

"We'll get them out," Hunter echoed Adam's earlier words fiercely.

Kylie pulled back a little and wiped at her eyes furiously.

"You're damn right we're going to get them out!" she growled.

Hunter settled himself back into his seat and turned on the ignition. "Let's go talk to Maxim. We'll decide what to do next from there, though I have a feeling none of us will be getting much sleep tonight."

***

The utterly blank look on Maxim's face when he met

them at the door to his office at Southern Glacier and the way he immediately fixed his eyes on her sent every alarm bell in Kylie's head screeching. She recalled that he had left the clinic in order to view some new video footage. The scents coming off him were also strange, and once again, she cursed her ignorance.

"It's about Molly, isn't it?" she blurted out before they could even step into the room.

Maxim stilled completely for a breath, that small hesitation making her anxiety levels skyrocket.

"Your perception's pretty good," he replied as he stepped aside and waved them inside. "That or my poker face is slipping."

Kylie grabbed one of his arms. "What did you find?"

"A connection, possibly." He sighed. "I had hoped to investigate it a little more before discussing it with you, but maybe showing you the footage will be better."

"Footage?" Hunter questioned. "Are we talking security footage from a business or from one of your people's personal cameras?"

"It's security footage from Riverford Regional. A guy from my clan works security for them, and I asked him to review their footage from the last couple of days, particularly keeping an eye out for all the people we've been able to identify to be likely Sniffers. It seems our two cougar friends Lana's been tailing have shown up an alarming number of times in the footage, but it's what they did there today that's so troubling."

Maxim walked over to his desk and picked up his phone. After scrolling through a few pictures, he handed the phone to Kylie. "These are the two cougars we've been watching as probable Sniffers."

The picture was of two blond men who looked to be in their late twenties. They didn't look even remotely familiar.

While she was staring at the picture, Maxim turned his large, flat-paneled monitor around so they could all see it. Hunter and she moved to stand at the edge of his desk. A video player window was open and paused on a grainy scene of what Kylie instantly recognized as the waiting area of Riverford Regional's ER. Before she could scrutinize it further, Maxim reached over to the touchscreen and dragged the slider bar back a few frames with his finger.

"Watch the entrance carefully."

Frowning, Kylie bent closer. Within a minute, two light-haired men walked in, and her eyes narrowed as she stared at their faces. Even a bit grainy, she recognized them as the cougars in the picture.

Kylie felt Hunter stir beside her. "This was just a few hours ago. Still looking for Kylie's father, maybe? Or the assassin?"

"Maybe yes to all of that," Maxim said, his eyes glued to the screen, "but in a few seconds you'll see— well, just watch."

Kylie could practically taste the tension coming off the tiger, but she didn't dare take her eyes off the unfolding scene to see his expression.

The two men made their way to the nurses' station where they paused to talk to a couple of the nurses working behind the long counter. One of the nurses nodded and walked off while one of the men continued to talk to the remaining nurse. The other leaned up against the counter with his back towards her, his posture casual.

Suddenly, Kylie gasped as the nurse returned and she got a good look at the person wearing regular street clothes trailing her. No—it couldn't be...

"I was under the impression that Karen Wilson and her son had gone into hiding," Maxim said grimly.

Each of his words was like a pebble falling into a still pond, and yet she still found herself shaking her head, rejecting the horrible direction her mind wanted to go. There was no way—*no way* Karen would betray them! It had to be a horrible coincidence. She probably had no idea those two were Sniffers. She looked at Hunter pleadingly, but the expression on his face mirrored his friend's.

"There's no *way* Karen's working for the lions!"

Kylie protested vehemently. "Her *husband* was murdered by a lion, for God's sake!"

Maxim nodded. "That was my exact thought—at first." He paused the video and moved it back a few seconds. "Watch."

The last thing Kylie wanted to do was watch, but she forced herself not to look away, to not even blink as someone she had always thought of like an aunt immediately gestured for the two Sniffers to follow after her without so much as a moment's hesitation or hint of wariness in her demeanor. Karen was as relaxed as if she was talking to a couple of friends. Even if Karen had a good reason for being in the ER at the moment instead of hiding away—Mitch *had* been injured after all and maybe they had lied about how serious it was in order to not add to her worries—what she was seeing now was pretty damning.

When the trio walked out of the camera's view, Maxim paused the video. Kylie felt Hunter slip a comforting arm around her waist, but her eyes remained fixed on the scene frozen on the screen, unable to face either man and see the pity that was very likely in their eyes just yet.

"Grief is a terrible thing," Maxim said into tense silence. "It changes a person's entire perspective. Imagine if a loved one was killed and those same murderers went on to threaten another, this time a child.

You'd be more likely to believe them when they say the knife is already pressed against that child's throat."

Kylie looked at him sharply. "You're saying they might have *blackmailed* her, threatened to kill Mitch?"

"I did find it strange that the assassin found you and your father so quickly, and after seeing this footage and the history of the Wilson family being what it is, I'm almost certain of it."

"Is this all the footage of them you have?" Hunter asked.

"They pop up in a few other feeds. One shows her entering an employee lounge briefly while the cougars wait outside. The others show them leaving the hospital, and then the premises, on foot."

Hunter turned Kylie's body to face him. "Did you tell Karen or Mitch the location of my clan's clinic?" he asked, his voice suddenly urgent.

"No," she replied with relief, realizing what he was really asking. "I didn't think that was something I should blab about without permission, so I just told her you brought us somewhere safe and hidden where Paul could be treated."

"Speaking of safe and hidden," Maxim said, "I'm pretty shocked that you allowed Kylie to leave the clinic."

"I didn't have a choice," Hunter replied irritably. "The wolf clan Elders wanted to talk face-to-face, but before I could leave, Gaither cornered us. He wanted to talk to Kylie. There was no way I was going to leave her there, so Kylie made up an excuse about needing to fetch something important for her father and we blew him off. Until we find out for sure whether or not there's another Polyshifter running around River-ford, she stays with either me or you at all times."

"My people have found nothing new on that front," Maxim said, flashing Kylie an apologetic ex-pression. "Unfortunately, there were no shifters living in your friend, Molly's, apartment complex, so there were no witnesses to even ask about whether or not any gators had been seen lurking in the last day or so. All we can do now is scour the city and try to pick up Molly's scent while the police investigate as they usu-ally do. Your friend, Tara, was sent home about thirty minutes ago, and I sent a couple of my wolves to keep an eye on her place tonight."

"Saying 'thanks' just doesn't seem like enough," Kylie said guiltily. "I just wish I could do more to help, especially now that I found out—oh! I still haven't told you! It's the reason why we came to talk to you in the first place. I might have finally found my mother!"

CHAPTER EIGHTEEN

"Your mother?" Maxim echoed, looking completely taken aback.

Kylie nodded. "When we went to see Jack and the wolf Elders, he freaked out when he saw me. He said I looked like one of the cougars that were being held captive at that horrible ranch, that her name was Grace. If you saw a picture of my mother during her college days, you would probably think it's me, we look that much alike. Also, my mother's name is Grace, and ever since she came here to America, she's lived as a cougar."

She looked at both men with determination. "That's why whatever you two plan on doing to rescue the captives, count me in."

"No!" Hunter practically snarled, his arm tightening around her waist as though he expected her to run off right then and there. "If you think I would let you within a hundred miles of that place—"

Kylie's eyes narrowed. "Don't even think about trying to keep me out of it. At the very least, if you plan to storm the place, I can bring my lion soul to the forefront, serve as a distraction."

"That cougar may not be your mother," Hunter argued.

"Doesn't matter," Kylie replied mulishly. "Your brother and Anna definitely *are* there, and if I can help in any way, I want to do it."

"I hate to say it," Maxim cut in, "but she does have a good point. A lion may even get us through the front door, so to speak."

Hunter shot his best friend a look of betrayal. "If her mother really is one of their captives, her cover would be blown the moment anyone in that place got a good look at her."

Kylie shrugged. "I'll wear a blonde wig."

This time Kylie was on the receiving end of his withering gaze. "I don't want to lose someone else that I care about to those fuckers if things go south."

Her heart thumped painfully at his admission. Dammit, but the look of very real pain in his eyes made her want to give in, to allow him to protect her completely as he had promised earlier. She smiled at him sadly and bent over to kiss him softly, not caring that Maxim was watching. She had never been the type of person to sit around and let others take care of her if she could at all help it, and this time would be no different no matter how long Hunter looked at her with those pleading eyes.

"And I don't want to lose you, either," she said softly, "but this is something I have to do for myself just as much as you do. If that cougar really is my mother—I would never forgive myself if something went wrong and I knew I didn't do everything in my power to help get her out of there."

Hunter sighed and pressed his forehead firmly against her own. "Why is it that I only seem to attract stubborn people into my life?" he said, his tone tinged with amusement.

The smile that Maxim directed at them was bittersweet. "Well, *somebody* needs to kick your brooding ass into shape when I'm not around."

Hunter snorted but he didn't deny it. Kylie supposed she needed his reticence just as much. They really did complement each other, she thought with some surprise.

"Hopefully we'll have a lot more intel on the ranch and what the fuck those sickos are actually doing there by the morning," Maxim said, "and in the meantime, let's see just how many shifters on this end are willing to follow us into what very well may turn out to be a serious battle. With all these Sniffers and assassins suddenly coming out of the woodwork, I really don't think we should wait longer than another day to make our move, be it covert or all-out war."

"The wolf clan Elders are waiting for me to go back," Hunter said. "I'll see just how far they're willing to go. Afterwards, I'll contact some friends from the bobcat clan and see if I can drudge up some volunteers."

Maxim shook his head. "I seriously doubt you'll have to try all that hard," he said dryly.

"I'm counting on it."

Maxim turned to her and said, "Kylie, if Karen calls you, don't answer. Wait an hour, then text her a message saying that you and your father are okay but in the process of being moved to a new, undisclosed location and will call her as soon as you're settled. If she *is* being coerced, that'll buy them some safety for a few days and us some time to locate both her and Mitch. I'll see if I can get some of the shifters on the force to pick them up once we do find them. Innocent or not, we need to confront her with the security footage sooner rather than later."

Kylie nodded.

"I may need to call you later for a three-way conference with the wolves, so keep your phone handy," Hunter said as he took Kylie's hand and led her to the door. "Unless something else comes up, we'll be at my clan's clinic once I finish talking with the wolves."

"Stay safe, you two."

"Bobcats?" Kylie asked Hunter skeptically as they left Maxim's club through the VIP exit. Although only a couple of Maxim's employees were around, she still lowered her voice. "Going against a lion, I imagine it would be like David and Goliath."

Hunter grinned. "That's not a bad comparison. It's not their claws or fangs I'm interested in, it's their guns."

Kylie looked at him incredulously. "Guns…?"

"That whole clan practically worships anything with a loud bang. Civil War era firearms, cannons, AK47s, all the way down to fireworks, they're crazy about them all. A few of them have even medaled in both men's and women's shooting in the Olympics over the years. Having an opportunity to participate in an actual gunfight would literally be a dream come true for most of them."

"Do you really think it'll come to that?" Kylie asked worriedly.

"I truly hope not, but we need to be prepared for the worst case scenario. Having a few sharpshooters in our corner can only better our chances."

Once inside the truck, Kylie rubbed at her eyes wearily. "I wonder if I should even tell Paul about any of this—Karen, the ranch, a new, very promising lead on my mother. He has enough on his plate dealing with his injury as it is." She paused. "I planned on leaving him behind, you know. If we would have made it to England, I was going to leave him, maybe even that same day. You see, even if we managed to find my mother's clan and they accepted me back into the fold, there was no way they would have allowed a human to live among them. With my secret out, my life in Riverford was pretty much over, but Paul still had his practice, his friends. He was *human*. He had already given up so much to raise me that I just…"

Kylie trailed off and shrugged, unable to put the rest of what she was feeling into words.

"But now you're *here*," Hunter said firmly. "It doesn't have to be an either/or decision. If there's a silver lining to be found in that lioness attacking you, it's that our Elders know your father's no longer in the dark about shifters without revealing that he knew about us all along. You *both* can be a part of the jaguar clan now. You don't have to give him up. For what it's worth, now that Paul has both feet planted into our world, I don't think he should be kept out of the loop.

He needs to understand the danger completely in order to keep himself safe. As much as I hope this latest mess with the lions'll be resolved within the next few days, it could very well go on for years. We can't keep him hidden away forever. That's no way to live."

Kylie slumped in her seat. "The more I try to protect him, the more it seems I make things worse."

Hunter reached over and squeezed her hand. "If my brother's disappearance taught me anything, it's that we don't have as much control over our lives as we think, but now you'll have a whole clan to help you through those inevitable rough patches if that's what you ultimately decide you want when or if this current mess is all over."

To be a jaguar for the rest of her life… The implications of that thought were something she wasn't ready to face just quite yet, and she was grateful to Hunter for understanding that about her.

She gave into the urge to kiss him, leaning over and pressing her lips against the lush softness of his own in a caress that was all affection and she hoped, full of meaning.

"Thank you," she murmured as she drew back, offering him a small smile even as the answering affection so blatantly visible in his eyes made her heart ache.

She really didn't deserve a man like him.

"We should get going," Hunter said a bit gruffly,

releasing her hand in order to reach for the ignition. "I'd really like to get tonight's business finished as soon as possible so you can get some rest. That's one promise to your father I'm determined to keep."

Kylie shook her head in amusement. "As long as you plan on getting some sleep along with me, I think I can help you with that."

CHAPTER NINETEEN

"I'm sorry about that," Hunter said as they left the wolf clan's secret den a couple of long hours later, his voice still tight with suppressed anger.

"It's okay, really," Kylie insisted. "We knew they had questions for me. It's not really surprising that they thought I could help 'awaken' some of their Deadends."

"It was beyond rude to put you on the spot like that, even worse to bring out that little boy. I just hope to God they didn't tell the kid why they wanted you to take a look at him. Having his hopes crushed like that would've been too cruel."

"I would say their timing was just as bad given the reason we were even there, but they probably thought it would be their only chance to ask and went for it.

Being a former Deadend myself, I can understand the parents' desperation."

Kylie couldn't help but think that it was a good thing Hunter was such a naturally calm person. They needed the strength and unique talents of the wolf clans, and storming out in anger, no matter how justified, would have been an utter disaster. As far as she was concerned, a little discomfort on her part was well worth the numbers the wolf Elders had pledged for the rescue in the end.

"I suppose so," Hunter said with a sigh. "It's just, you didn't see the stricken look on your face. As if you didn't have enough shit to deal with already."

"Well, maybe now the fact that I can't magically trigger an awakening will make the gossip rounds, and I won't ever have to deal with that awkward scene again." She broke off as a yawn threatened to split her face in two. "Are we going to see your bobcat friends now?"

"No. We're going back to the clinic. For now, I can just talk to them over the phone. We can just meet with them in the morning if it becomes necessary, or have them meet us at Southern Glacier."

Kylie hoped that none of her relief showed. She was currently running on fumes, but she would have sooner cut her own tongue off than complain.

Once they arrived back to the clinic, Kylie insisted

on peeking in on a still-sleeping Paul before allowing Hunter to usher her up to the room they had made love in what felt like years ago instead of hours.

She had been more than a little worried that Donald Gaither would be waiting to ambush them, but the Elder was nowhere to be seen, and nobody had stopped them to relay a message on their way up. It seemed they had managed to avoid that potential landmine for the time being, but she couldn't help but worry that their evasive behavior was making him suspicious. The last thing she needed right now was to make the Elders want to look more closely at her past more than they already were. She didn't want Hunter or Maxim in the middle of that kind of fallout.

After changing into her nightgown, Kylie climbed onto the bed and slipped beneath the sheets to snuggle against Hunter. He had stripped down to just his t-shirt and boxers and was already propped against the headboard and talking on the phone to what was probably one of his bobcat friends. Without missing a beat, he slipped an arm around her and pulled her snug against his side. Kylie wrapped an arm around his middle and used his chest as a pillow. It was almost scary how good it felt to simply be held like this, how *right*, but luckily she was too exhausted to scrutinize her feelings. She closed her eyes with a sigh. She could always freak out about it in the morning.

***

"Time to wake up."

The words sounded as though they had been spoken somewhere in the far distance, but they were enough to jolt Kylie out of a dream that involved arguing with a group of people whose identities were already beginning to elude her. She was incredibly warm and comfortable and was loathe to move, but she had never been one to allow herself the indulgence of lounging in bed, not when there was always, *always* something that needed to be done.

However, the moment her eyes cracked open and a very familiar face blurred into view only a few inches from her own, she was suddenly wide awake.

"Did something happen?" she asked anxiously, pulling away in order to sit up, somewhat wobbly, onto her knees. Her eyes immediately zeroed in on the cell phone in his hand.

"Needles just texted me," Hunter replied as he sat up as well. "Your father's awake and asking for you."

"Is he okay?"

Hunter nodded. "I think he was just worried about your current whereabouts. This floor has a communal bathroom if you'd like to get cleaned up before seeing him. I can check in with Maxim while you shower."

Kylie's eyes fell to the clock on the nightstand on Hunter's side of the bed. Eight AM. She'd slept longer than she had thought.

"I fell asleep while you were still talking to your bobcat friends," she said as she walked over to grab one of the duffle bags sitting on the dresser. "I hope things went well."

Hunter snorted. "As Maxim predicted, they were more than happy to help. We can expect at least twenty shooters from their clan. After we visit with your father, we'll head over to the club again to go over any new intel and start planning the next step."

Twenty minutes later, Kylie was showered and drying her hair as Hunter took his turn in the bathroom. She glanced over at one of Paul's bags, wondering if she should take it to him now, when Hunter's phone abruptly rang. She stared at it for only a second or two before she ran to the nightstand where he had left it and scooped it up. It was Maxim's name on the screen, so she decided to answer.

"Kylie?" Maxim said hesitantly after her greeting.

"Yeah," she replied. "Hunter's in the shower right now. Should I go fetch him?"

"No, no," he said, a little too quickly. "Just have him call me when he gets out."

Kylie was instantly on high alert. "Maxim—if it's

something bad, just say so. You don't have to tiptoe around me, especially if the bad news has to do with me."

Silence greeted her for a long moment, then she heard him sigh. "Fine, but I would rather tell you in person. Don't bother to have Hunter call me. Just come to the club as soon as you can."

"We will, and thanks, Maxim."

"What will we do?" Hunter suddenly said from directly behind her, nearly causing her to jump out of her skin for what seemed like the millionth time in the last twenty-four hours. She had been so focused on the call that she hadn't even heard the door open.

She whirled around. "God, don't sneak up on me like that!" she scolded.

"A strange thing to say for a jaguar," he remarked with a shake of his head.

"I don't think so. I'm still getting used to being a shifter, after all," Kylie huffed defensively.

"Of course," he agreed affably. "What did Maxim want?"

"Something's happened, but he didn't want to tell me what over the phone. He said to come to the club as soon as possible."

Hunter sat on the bed and began pulling on his boots. "Then we'll just go talk to your dad and leave straight after. I had hoped we would have time for breakfast, but I guess we'll just have to grab something on the way." He looked at her sternly. "I *know* you haven't eaten anything in a while. I would rather we not face any more disasters today on an empty stomach."

Kylie made a face. "The thought of eating, even now, is—ugh—but I'll try."

The clinic's halls were virtually empty as they made their way down to her father's floor. Seeing Paul's face light up the moment they stepped into his room made Kylie instantly feel guilty. She really shouldn't have left him alone last night, but...

"You're looking so much better," she said, leaning down to give him a careful hug.

He laughed. "I actually don't feel too bad, all things considered. I'm just a little tender. I'm glad to see you looking more rested than I expected." His eyes flickered over to Hunter who was standing silently behind her. "Thank you for taking care of my daughter last night."

Hunter shook his head. "No thanks needed."

"On the contrary. Kylie can be quite stubborn," Paul said, looking at her fondly.

Kylie flashed Paul a look of outrage, which quickly transferred to Hunter at the sound of his laughter.

She sank into the chair beside his bed. "If you two are quite finished teasing me, I have something serious to tell you."

The amusement in Paul's eyes instantly vanished. "Did something else happen?" he demanded. "Is Karen and Mitch all right?"

Kylie mentally winced. She had hoped to put off telling him about Karen's possible betrayal just a little longer.

"They're not hurt," she replied slowly. "At least I don't think they are, but something—unsettling has come up." She paused, unsure how she should tell him.

Hunter placed a hand on her shoulder and squeezed gently. "Before that, you might want to explain about your friend, Molly, and the possible ties to your attack," he suggested.

Kylie flashed him a grateful smile and turned back to Paul when he said in a surprised tone, "Molly?"

"Tara called me last night," she said grimly. "Someone broke into Molly's apartment, and she, and maybe even Ty, are missing. Hunter asked some of the shifters on the police force to investigate, and they found some spatters of blood and the smell of an alligator shifter inside her apartment. Hunter's friend, Maxim, has some of his people looking for her, too, but so far they haven't found any other leads."

Paul ran a hand agitatedly through his hair. "I've never heard of any alligators allying with *any* clan, much less the lions, but the timing is much too suspicious to be coincidental."

"If the lions *are* behind her abduction, then I suspect we'll be hearing from them soon," Hunter said. "It may be a ploy to get Kylie to reveal herself. That lioness came after her because she thought Kylie was a rogue lion, and the lion clans hunt Rogues just as relentlessly as they do Polyshifters and the families that flee their tyranny."

Paul frowned. "And you think the lions are now targeting Karen and Mitch in the same way?" He reached out and grabbed Kylie's upper arm urgently. "Have they already been attacked again? Is that what you're trying to tell me?"

Kylie squirmed under his intense, worried gaze. "I—" She broke off and exchanged a troubled glance with Hunter. Despite that damning security video, she really couldn't say for certain if Karen had *not* been attacked and delivered an ultimatum before the scene in the hospital occurred. For all they knew, the lions may have already kidnapped Mitch, too. She suddenly realized that they just didn't have enough evidence either way to completely condemn or exonerate Karen.

"I'm not sure," she admitted, feeling Hunter start beside her. She hastened to explain before Hunter could speak, "When I last talked to her, she told me that Mitch was doing fine and they had gone into hiding, but…Maxim knows a shifter who works security at Riverford Regional. He sent some footage from yesterday afternoon to Maxim that shows Karen meeting up with two men, cougars, that have been identified as probable Sniffers. Her body language was pretty relaxed, like she was talking to a couple of friends. She left the hospital with them on foot."

Paul's fingers went lax around her arm. His expression was stricken. "She would never…after what happened to Steven…!"

"That's the very reason she would," Hunter said quietly, his eyes sympathetic, "but Kylie's right. At this point, we don't know nearly enough about what we saw to condemn her. Maxim's people are trying to locate her and Mitch as we speak. In fact, Maxim called this morning wanting us to meet him to discuss something important. For all I know, it could be something about the Wilsons."

"Then you should go see him, now," Paul said firmly. "Kylie, just promise me that you'll call me the moment you hear something, *no matter how bad.*"

"I will," she promised solemnly.

"And for God's sake, be careful! I don't want you coming back here on a stretcher—either of you."

It wasn't until they were on their way to Southern Glacier that Kylie realized with dismay that she had

completely forgotten to tell Paul about the very promising lead Jack had given her on her mother. He was
so going to kill her, but it was too late to go back now.

CHAPTER TWENTY

After stopping for a few breakfast burritos and coffee at a nearby cafe, Kylie found herself once again following Hunter into Maxim's club. Without the loud thrum and pulsing of the club's music filling the air, the empty halls felt a little disconcerting and forlorn.

From the rumpled state of Maxim's clothes, the same ones he had worn last night she was quick to note, the tiger shifter had either slept in his office or not at all. His eyes certainly looked tired enough to be the latter.

Hunter handed Maxim one of his bags of food and one of the coffees as Kylie sank down into one of the chairs in front of the desk. "You look like shit. I hope you at least got a couple of hours of sleep."

Maxim sighed wearily. "I stretched out on one of the couches upstairs for two or three once we closed the club, but then the phone calls started to come in."

"You can eat and talk about the latest disaster at the same time," Hunter said, looking pointedly at the still-unopened bag in Maxim's hand. He sat down next to Kylie and began pulling burritos out of his bag and placing them on the desk. He pushed a couple towards Kylie. "That goes for you, too."

Maxim chuckled and complied, moving to sit behind his desk. "Thanks." He unwrapped his burrito and took a couple of bites before fixing his eyes on Kylie. "As you know, I have several of my friends that live in the Panhandle region watching the ranch along with the wolves their Elders sent. One of them called me about an hour ago to report that a couple of SUVs entered the property." He turned his monitor around to face them. "Here's the pics he sent me of the people getting out of one of them."

Kylie experienced a moment of dread before she put down her food and focused on the screen. Unlike the slightly fuzzy security footage she had viewed yesterday, this picture was sharp and clear in all its horrifying detail. The image was of the back of a fairly ordinary two-story brick house with an attached four-car garage. Two black SUVs were parked side-by-side in front of the still-closed garage door. There were four people standing next to the left-most vehicle, three of them men with the fourth a *very* familiar redheaded woman clutched between them.

"Oh my God, *Molly*," Kylie whispered in horror.

She could just make out that her friend's hands were bound behind her back as well as the expression of absolute fear on her face. Conspicuously absent was her boyfriend Ty. Rather than feel relieved, her dread doubled. If they had not kidnapped him, too, then where was he? She couldn't imagine that Tara or the cops wouldn't have been able to get ahold of him by now if he had just forgotten to charge his phone.

"My security guys questioned the lioness into unconsciousness as soon as I saw the pictures and made the connection," Maxim said, his eyes hard, "and still not a word. Even so, with this, there is no longer any question. The lions have infiltrated Riverford far deeper than we feared. I imagine Kylie will be receiving an ultimatum, most likely through Karen Wilson, soon."

Kylie didn't think it was possible, but his eyes hardened even more until she could barely see the blue of his irises. The tiger shifter was *pissed*, dangerously so. She could taste his desire to rend, to *kill*, in the air, and she suddenly had to grab the arms of her chair tightly as her muscles rippled and the urge to shift almost overwhelmed her. She wasn't sure, but she thought she might have hissed as well.

"We have to make our move before that happens."

Hunter's calm proclamation washed over her, as out of place and potent as a clap of thunder in a silent room. The small spasms in her muscles that she had been struggling against ceased in response to the calm he was projecting. She felt his hand glide over hers in a soothing motion, and the urge to shift also began to fade.

She took a shuddering breath and smiled at Hunter gratefully, but he wasn't looking at her. His eyes were fixed on Maxim, intense, watchful. It was then that Kylie realized with a sinking feeling that the taste, the smell of violence was still very much present. She stilled, almost afraid to even breathe, as the two alpha predators stared at each other, each as still as a marble statue.

Then Maxim blinked, and the suffocating tension in the air seemed to dissipate all at once.

"I'm okay, now," he said roughly, though his eyes still smoldered with anger.

Hunter nodded. "Your tiger'll get his chance. Both of us will get our taste of blood soon."

Although his words should have disturbed her, something deep inside of her understood them well, wanted to join them, even. Kylie hastily pushed those feelings to the side. It was best to deal with them later, when she wasn't so on edge and in danger of losing herself to her jaguar. Hunter and Maxim had enough to deal with without having to chase after a rampaging Returner.

Maxim took a deep breath and let it out slowly. "Call the bobcats and the wolf Elders and have them come to the club. I think it's time to plan an infiltration of our own."

***

Still reeling from the discovery that Molly, minus Ty, was now a prisoner in a place that had done unspeakable things to God-only-knew how many others, Kylie sat silently beside Hunter on one of the many couches in one of the VIP sections of Southern Glacier and listened while the large group of assembled shifters strategized.

"One of my guys has managed to learn the identity of one of their scientists, a geneticist from the LA lion clan," Maxim said, bringing up a photo of a blond man who looked to be around sixty onto the flatscreen on the wall before them. "He's also learned where the lion stays within Amarillo when he is not at the ranch."

"I recognize the bastard," one of the wolf Elders

from Parker Grove spoke up. "He was in the news not too long ago—something about analyzing the mitochondrial DNA in some recently discovered Denisovan bones."

"If they're mucking about with DNA, do you suppose they are trying to develop some kind of biological weapon at that ranch?" another wolf asked. "Something that is only affective on shifters?"

Maxim's expression hardened. "That's the very reason why this needs to be an infiltration rather than an all-out assault. We need to do this as quietly and covertly as possible to not only give us a chance to rescue our loved ones unharmed, but to also steal as much of their data as we can get our hands on. The last thing we want is to go in guns blazing…" He leveled a *look* at the group of bobcats. "…and risk them killing all their captives and destroying all their data. We need to be inside the complex and down in the lower levels before they even realize they're being invaded. We'll back them into a corner of our choosing. While rescuing our people will be our priority, we need to find out what the bastards are up to just as badly, especially now that we're finding more and more of the bastards in our city."

"We can use the geneticist as our distraction," Hunter said, looking meaningfully at Kylie, "catch him as he's heading back to the ranch and use his vehicle.

We can have the bobcats take out all the perimeter guards simultaneously with tranqs while their attention is turned to the geneticist's arrival."

Maxim nodded. "I can also have some of my guys hack into their security system. It should buy us enough time to get a couple of rescue teams inside. I wasn't able to locate any schematics, so we'll be moving pretty much blind from that point on. We only have the intel Jack Bray has provided us of the interior and its personnel. We've constructed a partial floor-plan based on what Jack's recollected."

The picture of the geneticist was replaced with the ranch's partially constructed floorplans. Kylie frowned as she noticed several underground floors. How in the world were they ever going to find all the captives, much less rescue them from such a structure, especially when they had such a small window of time to do it?

"One last thing." Suddenly a picture of Molly Maxim had probably swiped from one of her social media accounts appeared on the flat-screen next to the ranch's floorplan. "This woman's name is Molly Johnson, one of the lions' most recent victims. Although human, she is a friend of Kylie Moore's and was taken, we think, to use as a bargaining chip."

Suddenly all eyes were on Kylie. She could feel her back stiffen as she struggled not to fidget. Maybe it wasn't such a good idea to remind everyone that she was a Returner. There were a lot of different clans present, most with shifters she had never met. She didn't want a repeat of the awkwardness she'd had to endure last night with the wolves once the meeting was over.

"As you well know," Maxim continued, capturing everyone's attention again to Kylie's relief, "the lions have always coveted Returners. Thus, it's crucial that we relieve the bastards of such a precious coin. Also, before Molly was taken, she wasn't aware of the existence of shifters, so use caution when approaching her should her ignorance still be true. The last thing we need to throw into the mix is a terrified, hysterical human who thinks the tiger or wolf trying to save her is there to eat her."

"Which city and location are our various groups to meet up?" the wolf Elder, Glen, asked.

"Lubbock," Maxim replied. "I will be flying in ahead with a few people as soon as our business here is concluded in order to meet with my contacts who live in the area and to start coordinating our attack. One of my cousins has an estate on several hundred acres on the western outskirts of the city. It is remote and will draw no attention as it's located on a private hunting range and often hosts large groups. We'll discuss our final plans in more detail once everyone has arrived at the estate."

"Are we going with Maxim?" Kylie whispered into Hunter's ear as several people began to ask Maxim a few more questions.

"Yes," Hunter whispered back. "He has a private plane, a six-seater Cessna."

"He has a pilot's license?" she asked, impressed.

Hunter nodded. "Everyone in his family does. It's a tradition."

Movement in the corner of her eye had Kylie instinctually turning her head. A young, blonde girl that could have been anywhere between sixteen and twenty was striding towards Maxim, a harried look on her face. Kylie caught the scent of tiger as she passed by their couch with a curt nod to Hunter and a curious glance at her.

Maxim instantly stiffened when he caught sight of her. She stepped right up to him and began whispering into his ear.

"Who is she?" Kylie asked.

Hunter's smile was half amusement, half worry. "That's Sasha, Maxim's little sister."

CHAPTER TWENTY-ONE

Kylie felt Sasha's stare like a physical touch as she and Hunter approached the tiger siblings after the rest of the shifters left to make preparations to travel west. Blatantly sizing her up, it made the jaguar in Kylie want to growl in warning. To distract herself from inadvertently doing something embarrassing, she focused on the warmth of Hunter's hand around hers and tried to make her expression as friendly and open as possible.

Maxim glanced at his sister, probably sensing the slight tension between them, and said, "That's right. You two haven't been introduced yet. Sasha, this is Kylie Moore, Kylie, this is my little sister, Sasha."

Kylie held out her hand with a small smile and was relieved when the girl's scrutinizing gaze melted into a grin as she accepted Kylie's hand for a shake. "Nice to meet you, Kylie. I'm glad to see Hunter has finally found a strong woman that'll cheer his brooding ass up. Except for the night he brought you here and you started that brawl, he hasn't been in the club except to talk business with Max in ages. I haven't seen him that animated since he and my brother used to pick fights with the Bengals or the bears back in high school."

"Um…" Kylie had no idea how to respond to that, looking at first Hunter and then Maxim with a raised eyebrow. "You picked fights?"

Hunter, however, shot Sasha a dirty look. "Just because I don't like crowds doesn't mean I brood. And we didn't 'pick fights,' either."

Maxim's grin was nearly identical to his sister's. "No, we just finished them." Then his expression sobered. "And we sure as hell will finish this one."

Sasha's eyes suddenly became fierce. "We'll get Anna back, Max. Ryder and Kylie's friend, too. We'll make those bastards pay for even thinking they could touch our own without severe consequences."

"You're coming with us?" Kylie asked.

The blonde girl nodded, then threw a challenging look at Maxim. "I'll be flying the plane. The last thing Max needs is to be exhausted once we reach Lubbock. Our older brother and my mate can run things here just fine while we're gone."

Maxim threw up his hands. "Fine. You can fly us there, *but*, I don't want you anywhere near that damned ranch."

"I don't have a death wish, Max," Sasha huffed. "I'm not nearly as good a fighter as any of you, but I want to do my part in helping Anna. I love her, too, you know."

Kylie shifted uncomfortably, suddenly feeling as if she was eavesdropping on a conversation not meant for outside ears.

"Hey, we're going to head out, you two," Hunter said, breaking the awkward mood, to Kylie's relief. "We need to grab a few things for the trip."

Maxim nodded. "Meet us at the airport in an hour, same hanger as always."

"We'll talk more later, Kylie," Sasha said, something like a conspiratorial gleam in her eyes. Kylie could well imagine the stories she could tell her about Hunter.

A slow smile stretched her lips. "I look forward to it."

"I just knew the two of you would get along," Hunter said with a heavy sigh as they drove away from the club. "She loves to tease, so expect to hear plenty about all our past exploits at the oddest times."

Kylie chuckled. "I could tell, though the way she was looking at me in the beginning, I half-expected her to go for my throat."

Another sigh. "She can be very protective, too. She's always treated me as one of her brothers. In this instance, I'm glad she insisted in coming along to take over pilot duties. Maxim needs the rest badly whether he'll admit it or not."

Kylie poked him in the side. "So do you. I can't imagine that you got more than a couple of hours yourself last night."

"It's only around an hour and a half flight from here to Lubbock, so I doubt any of us'll get much sleep on the plane, but I promise to sleep once we get to Maxim's cousin's estate. We'll need to be as rested and alert as possible should we decide to move on the ranch as early as tomorrow."

"This whole thing is almost surreal," Kylie said, shaking her head. "Last week I never would have thought I would be taking part in a military-like rescue operation."

"If we didn't need your ability to shift into a lion," Hunter said unhappily, "you wouldn't be getting any-where near that god-forsaken place at all."

"My best friend is in there and probably my mother," Kylie said heatedly. "Even if I couldn't shift into a lion, there's no way I would've let you leave me behind."

"Which brings us to the problem of your father,"

Hunter said. "Should we tell him what we're doing? I can't imagine that he'd be thrilled about you going directly into the lion's den, even if your mother *is* there."

"The condition he's in, I'd rather not upset him, but if something happens to me, I don't want him to blame you, either. He needs to at least know about what Jack said about the cougar shifter that looks like me."

Hunter reached over and squeezed her arm. "I won't let anything happen to you."

Kylie matched his determined expression. "We'll look out for each other."

She was still feeling more than a little guilty nearly an hour later as Hunter and she boarded Maxim's plane. She could still see the flash of panic in Paul's eyes when he had realized she meant to throw herself into the thick of things. He had spent a good portion of his life keeping her hidden away from the lions only to have her willingly enter into their domain in the end and knowing there wasn't a thing he could do to stop her from doing it, or worse, being *unable* to do anything about it, even join her, because he was currently stuck in a hospital bed.

"Promise me that you'll bring my little girl back to me."

The look in Paul's eyes when he had said that to Hunter was seared into her soul forever.

"The rest of the group are already on the road,"

Maxim informed them as they settled into the rear-most seats while the three wolves he had brought for their security filled the rest. He then gestured to the cell phone clutched tightly in Kylie's hand. "Has Karen tried to contact you yet? I'm sorry to say my people haven't been able to locate her or Mitch."

"No, and that fact really has me worried," Kylie replied.

"Maybe we should contact her first," Hunter suggested, "send her the text you mentioned earlier about Kylie and Paul being moved to a more secure location."

Maxim nodded. "Do it, and then turn your phone off until this whole mess is over. That goes for us, too. We can't be sure that they won't try to track them. We can buy a few pre-paid phones once we reach Lubbock."

"Fine by me. Gaither has already sent me over a dozen texts today," Hunter said with a grimace. "Needless to say, he's less than pleased that I'm ignoring him."

"I hope he doesn't start pestering Paul," Kylie fretted.

Hunter leaned over and kissed her forehead tenderly. "Your father took on a lion assassin without hesitation. Compared to that, taking on an Elder, even one as insufferable as Gaither, should be a piece of cake."

"The Elders are going to be so pissed when they find out we've left them out of all this," Kylie said.

"No doubt," Hunter agreed, "but we still have no idea about the identity of the gator who kidnapped your friend or even if it was a gator at all. Plus, with all the Sniffers suddenly popping up everywhere, even they will have to admit that keeping our rescue plans close to the chest was the smartest move here."

"That's enough yapping out of you three!" Sasha called from the front of the plane in a no-nonsense tone. "I offered to fly the plane to give you a chance to rest, Max, and I expect you to take it! Buckle up. We're about to take off."

Maxim sighed and turned to sit down in his seat properly without a word.

Hunter laced their hands together and looked at the back of Maxim's head with a faint smile.

Score one for Sasha.

CHAPTER TWENTY-TWO

Kylie brushed her lips lightly over Hunter's lips, making her lover scrunch his nose adorably as his eyes fluttered open. "We're here," she said.

Hunter blinked a few more times, then lifted his head from where it had been resting on Kylie's shoulder.

"I only meant to close my eyes for a few minutes," he said sheepishly.

Kylie smiled. "I'm sure that's what Maxim thought, but I think he drifted off the moment his eyes closed. I wish we didn't have to wake him up."

"Sasha will make sure he gets plenty of rest at the estate; I guarantee it. I'm actually glad she bullied him into allowing her to fly us here. She's really the only one that can force him to take care of himself sometimes."

Thirty minutes later, Kylie was shaking the hand of Maxim's cousin, Lev, a blond, handsome man in his mid-thirties and then they were climbing into his black Escalade. She ended up squished in between Hunter and Maxim in the backseat.

"Several of your men are waiting for you back at my place," Lev said as they left the airport. "Based on the intel I saw before I came out here to pick you all up, we should be able to draw up a pretty great battle map of the area. Josh also said that geneticist you're targeting left the ranch early this morning and headed into Amarillo. He currently has a couple of wolves staked out outside what appears to be his current residence."

"Good. We should probably expect the first people we recruited to start arriving in four to five hours," Maxim said.

"I've got the large hunting lodge on the west field ready to accommodate them," Lev said. "You all can stay in the main house." Kylie saw him grin in the rearview mirror. "Even the jaguar asshole in the back, but only because he has a lady with him."

"Thanks," Hunter said dryly, but he was grinning, too. To Kylie he added, "Lev's still sore about losing a friendly fight with me back when I was only thirteen."

"That's because I never expected you jaguars to be so sneaky!" the Siberian protested. "I was limping for two days after!"

Hunter snorted. "And whose fault is that?" he shot back, completely unrepentant.

"Really, Lev, give it a rest," Sasha said from the front seat. Although she could only see the girl's profile, Kylie imagined she was rolling her eyes at her cousin.

"So what kind of game do people hunt on his land?" Kylie asked.

"Deer, wild boars, some emu, nothing too exotic," Hunter replied.

"Are we talking about human hunters or shifters?"

"Both, but mostly shifters."

"My hunting packages are quite popular," Lev cut in. "Maybe when things aren't so dire, Hunter can bring you out for a weekend of hunting."

A surge of excitement washed through her at the thought of chasing down a deer. It was unsettling as she had never had the desire to hunt, even the human way. Now that her shifter side had awakened, she still wasn't sure she wanted to ever hunt, no matter what her instincts said about the matter. They hadn't yet revealed to Lev that she was a Returner, so he naturally assumed she had been hunting all her life like most shifters.

Sensing her discomfort, Hunter answered in her stead. "It may be way in the future, but yeah, sounds like something to look forward to."

They drove west out of the city about ten miles before turning down a dirt county road, the land dotted by mesquites on either side. Five minutes later, they stopped in front of a tall gate that blocked the entrance to another road, this one paved. Lev hopped out of the SUV to unlock and open the gate.

"His estate really is in the middle of nowhere," Kylie remarked as they began driving down the paved road and Lev's estate was still nowhere in sight.

"It's too remote for my tastes," Maxim said. "I like a little noise."

"Me, too," Sasha piped in.

"That's because you two are little hellions," Lev sniffed. "Cooped up in a building surrounded by hundreds of people night after night—*mingling*." He visibly shuddered. "Makes my skin crawl just thinking about it. I'm all about the fresh air and the sounds of nature."

When they crested a small incline, a large, three-story brick finally came into view in the distance.

"Wow, I wasn't expecting it to be so big," Kylie

blurted in a little awe. It was like seeing a resort in the middle of the Texas plains. She had thought they had been exaggerating when they said they were going to an "estate."

"Lev's younger brother and his mate also live there," Sasha said. "Taking into account his two sons and his niece, lots of space is necessary when it comes to tigers and their surly tempers."

At the estate, Kylie was briefly introduced to Lev's mate, Polina, their teenaged sons, and extended family before her group was shuffled into a large den with several couches that reminded her a bit of the community room down in the wolves' secret den. They then proceeded to spend the entire afternoon huddled around the half-finished map of the grounds and structures of the lions' ranch she had seen earlier, discussing possible strategies of attack, occasionally adding to the map as various people reported new intel to both Maxim and Lev as the day wore on.

After lunch, other shifters from Riverford began trickling in, the first to arrive were, unsurprisingly, the bobcats looking altogether too gleeful for such a dire situation, particularly the set of identical twin young men that Hunter spent a long while talking to. Apparently her lover had been friends with them since elementary school.

The last to arrive was Jack and his father. The injured wolf looked alarmingly pale and sickly. Although Kylie could understand only too well why he would refuse to be left behind, traveling in his condition had set his recovery back probably days. The way he looked now, as if he was a breath away from collapsing, she doubted he would be able to join them at the ranch at all, no matter how much he wanted to be there to see his mate rescued. Luckily Polina thought the same, and took it upon herself to fuss over him.

Through all this controlled chaos, and the dinner that followed, Kylie sat quietly beside Hunter, absorbing all the information and adding a suggestion a couple of times, but for the most part, she felt way out of her league in a discussion that resembled a military war council. As only Maxim and Hunter knew she was a Polyshifter, the very dangerous part she would play—that of an Assassin bringing urgent news, and probable punishment, about a possible breach in security with the geneticist as the suspect—was never mentioned, just that Maxim, Hunter, and a couple of wolves would handle that part of the operation.

Kylie felt sick when a photo of Molly was once again passed around, reminding everyone of the importance of rescuing the sole human among the captives and the precautions that absolutely needed to be taken. However, that was nothing close to the way her heart felt as though it had been shredded when Maxim began passing out copies of the photo she had given him of her mother that had been taken a week before her parents had left her with Paul and Laura.

As expected, almost everyone looked over at her with expressions of confusion. "My mother's been missing for over a decade," Kylie said quietly. "Her name is Grace Hall. Jack Bray thinks she may be one of the cougars being held captive."

Hunter slipped an arm around her waist and gave her a comforting hug. His familiar smell and the warmth of his body were enough to keep Kylie from losing it in front of everyone. After a couple of deep breaths, her pulse slowed back to a more normal rhythm.

"My cousin, Lev, has prepared a place for all of you to sleep in one of his hunting lodges," Maxim said into the following silence. "Jack, you and your father will obviously be staying here in the main house. We'll be heading out to Amarillo at the crack of dawn in order to get into position, so I suggest you get as much rest and sleep as possible."

"Follow me," Lev called out.

"I'll show the rest of you to your rooms," Polina said, waving over her sons to help Jack.

The kids had already taken their luggage up to the guestrooms on the second floor. The sky had just darkened, but even though it wasn't quite eight yet, Kylie suggested that she and Hunter go to bed, to which he readily agreed.

Kylie began rummaging in her bag that the kids had left on the bed for her nightgown and toiletries. She pointed towards the opened door of the *en suite* bathroom. "I'm just going to go wash up for bed," she said.

Hunter sat down on the bed and pulled out one of the throwaway cell phones Lev had given him. "I'll go in after you're done. I just need to make a call to the manager I left in charge of a couple of my complexes, first."

She couldn't resist bending down to give him a tender kiss. "I won't be long," she promised.

CHAPTER TWENTY-THREE

When Kylie entered the bedroom again, Hunter was standing at the sole window in the room wearing only his boxers, his eyes glazed and turned inward. The room was dark, illuminated only by the lights from the estate far below. The sky itself was an inky black with only a spattering of stars visible. Tonight was a new moon. Should tomorrow's circumstances force them to wait to make their move until nightfall, the added darkness could prove to be a lucky boon.

Kylie quietly walked over to him and slipped between him and the window, wrapping her arms around his bare torso. His entire body was so tense that it was almost like hugging a warm statue. This wouldn't do. At this rate, he would lie awake all night worrying about all the things that could go wrong tomorrow, fearing because of the things Jack had told him, that his brother was already dead and they would merely be recovering his body. He needed a distraction, and if she was being completely honest with herself, she needed a distraction just as badly.

She placed a deliberate, lingering kiss onto his neck, then another as he drew in a sharp, startled breath. Her fingertips teased up and down his spine as she continued to lightly kiss along his neck and shoulder before dipping both hands down to caress suggestively over the firm muscles of his ass.

If anything, his body became even more rigid, but he made no move to either embrace or push her away. She could almost sense his turmoil in the silence that remained over them, broken only by the sound of their accelerating heartbeats and breathing. The smell of his sudden arousal was potent, making the muscles throughout her entire body tighten in anticipation and her groin ache and throb.

He wanted her, but he wasn't sure he should allow himself the indulgence. She would have to push even harder.

"Help me forget how scared I am for everybody," Kylie murmured against his skin, pressing herself even harder against his body and tightening her arms around his waist. "Just for tonight."

She lifted up her head and raised herself on tip-toes to lightly touch her lips to his own. Then suddenly her back was being slammed against a wall, and Hunter's lips crashed against hers, kissing her as though he had been drowning and needed her mouth to breathe. He pushed his thighs between her legs until they opened to accommodate him. His hands moved roughly down her sides and slipped around her waist to grab her ass tightly, urging her to wrap a bare leg around his thigh as he ground his swollen member against the center of her pleasure almost desperately.

Kylie pushed back and rubbed herself against him just as aggressively, his mouth swallowing her moans as bursts of pleasure raced up her spine. Then suddenly his mouth was gone and her nightgown was being lifted over her head in one fell swoop before she could even open her eyes, the cool air within the room making her shiver as it hit her newly-bared skin.

Standing only in her panties, Kylie reached for Hunter's boxers and yanked them down his hips until they pooled at his ankles, her eyes fixed on his cock as it sprang free. The head was already darkened, wet and leaking, and she felt a surge of arousal in her groin that nearly had her knees buckling at the thought of it pounding into her until her mind and senses were filled with nothing but Hunter.

Before she could reach down to grasp his cock,

Hunter crushed her nearly-nude body against him, and his mouth dipped down to suck hungrily on her neck. Kylie gasped and trembled as Hunter worked one of her erogenous zones with lips, teeth, and tongue while her hardened nipples rubbed against his silky, slightly damp skin.

Hunter walked them back towards the bed and tumbled them onto the comforter. He watched with lust-filled eyes and something she couldn't quite identify as he pulled off her panties and she finally lay with her eyes hooded in lust and her cheeks flushed completely exposed like a sensual meal set out for his enjoyment.

He reached out a hand and began to caress down her body almost reverently rather than to inflame. "You're so beautiful," he said quietly, his eyes raising to fix intently on her face. "That you came into my life now of all times—I can't bear the thought of something happening to you. I want to lock you up in this room until all the danger has passed, but…"

Kylie swallowed thickly. "But I'm a Polyshifter, and the danger will *never* pass."

He nodded, his eyes infinitely sad, and he moved to cover her body with his own. "I know."

He kissed her gently, lovingly, with none of his earlier urgency present, and then for a long moment, he merely lay atop her, pressing his nose into her neck and inhaling her scent deeply. Kylie wrapped one arm around his back and up to grasp one shoulder tightly. The other hand, she slid into his hair, her fingertips cradling his head. Their legs seemed to intertwine naturally, and for a long moment, she just held him, their earlier, desperate ardor cooled but not completely gone. Just touching Hunter's skin was enough to send her own skin tingling, and his scent was still saturated with arousal, as evidenced by the hard cock trapped between their bodies.

She had thought to make his mind crazy with lust, but it seemed what Hunter needed more than to forget their worries, was to simply feel their connection. If they fell asleep intertwined just like this, then she would have no complaints. There would be plenty of time for them to make love once their loved ones were safe, and they would finally be able to explore their newly formed relationship at their leisure. She refused to believe otherwise.

Kylie listened to Hunter's soft breathing and the soothing rhythm of his heartbeat while softly caressing her fingers through his hair and lightly massaging his scalp. She had found it really soothing the times he had done the same for her. His weight was a pleasurable heaviness across her body, a warmth that soon had her drowsy and her eyes drooping.

Then suddenly Hunter shifted, and his hips thrust

forward, rubbing his hardness deliberately against the length of her wet folds. Kylie gasped, her drowsiness instantly gone, and instinctually tightened her thighs against his hips. He did it a second time, harder and more prolonged, and a soft moan escaped her throat as that silky hardness rubbed against her clit this time.

Hunter kissed her neck softly then lifted his head. Their eyes met, and Kylie could clearly see his love for her shining within them despite the darkness. It made her chest tighten painfully. None of the men she had dated had ever looked at her like that, like she was the only thing they could see or wanted to see.

Kylie raised her head and captured his lips, trying to put everything she was feeling, the slight fear, the happiness, and yes, even the love, into that one kiss. No tongue, just a passionate melding and rubbing of lips. When they broke apart, Kylie's cheeks felt warm, and her heart was racing to the point where she was beginning to feel slightly lightheaded.

The smile that stretched Hunter's lips was beautiful, happy and utterly belonging within that single moment. Then he lifted his body off hers slightly, holding himself aloft with one arm beside her head, and lowered his head to take one of her nipples into his mouth while he used his free hand to palm the other. Kylie immediately arched up against him, her skin hypersensitive from the emotions that last kiss had invoked.

Hunter took his time. He slowly lathed attention to one breast with his teeth, mouth, and tongue while he rolled and pinched the nipple of the other with varying degrees of pressure between his fingers. His eyes were closed as he did this, as if savoring the taste of her skin, but at the same time, his slow, deliberate actions were worshipful. All their previous lovemaking had been passionate, full of affection, yes, but there had always been something primal and wild to the way they had practically devoured each other.

Kylie had always thought it was because of their shifter nature, and maybe that was true, but the way he was caressing her body now was worlds different. It was deeper, perhaps even more passionate than getting totally lost in each other's bodies until all they could feel was the mind-numbing pleasure as they had before. Because this time she was just as aware of him and his reactions as she was of her own.

She tugged on his hair a bit and ran her fingernails lightly up and down his back until he shuddered. He released her breast from his mouth with a wet *pop* and surged up her body to take her lips again, licking almost lazily along the seam until she parted them and his tongue thrust forward to slide eagerly along her own.

His fingers brushed teasingly over her clit a few times, and Kylie bucked her hips in encouragement.

She was already wet and more than ready for him, the walls of her passage throbbing in anticipation of feeling his thick cock filling her so completely. She clutched at his buttocks, urging him forward as she arched her body into the caress.

Then his cock was suddenly pressing into her warmth in one, strong thrust that had Hunter swallowing her moans. She wrapped her legs around his hips and pressed him deeper inside with the heels of her feet. His hips began a slow roll as he pulled out almost completely and thrust into her with long, powerful strokes that allowed her to feel every inch of that silky hardness caress along her sensitive tissues.

As when he had been sucking on her breasts, Hunter seemed intent on savoring every clench of her passage and every cry wrenched from her throat when he angled his thrusts and rubbed against those most sensitive areas that drove her wild. There was nothing hurried or frenzied about his movements, no desperate need to reach the edge of the cliff, just a joy in the intimacy of it all. The pleasure was just a bonus.

Soon Kylie was thrusting back more forcefully in time to his rhythm, feeling the pressure in her groin building more keenly than ever before. A few more thrusts, and that pressure shattered into pure ecstasy, making her accidentally bite Hunter's bottom lip at the shock of it. She threw her head back with a moan as she rode out her climax, unable to keep her eyes open even though she ached to see his face as he found his own ecstasy.

Hunter allowed the full weight of his body to rest completely onto her as he gave a series of final deep thrusts, and the first spurts of his scorching seed began to fill her passage. She clamped her inner muscles down tightly on his cock, tearing an appreciative moan from his lips as he continued to thrust shallowly and jerkily into her soft warmth until he had been milked completely and fell still.

Kylie let her legs slip off his back and fall to either side of his hips. She playfully squeezed them against his slick flesh before raising her head for a kiss which he eagerly gave.

They didn't speak when they broke apart. Hunter withdrew from her and rolled them onto their sides. Kylie snuggled closer, pressing her face to his chest as he threw a leg over hers and his arms tightened around her waist.

For a long while, she listened to the steady beat of his heart and her slightly accelerated one until Hunter's breaths evened out into the rhythm of sleep that she had grown accustomed to in the last couple of days. Although their lovemaking had not been the wild and mind-numbing frenzy she had planned, she was nevertheless satisfied with the outcome in every way, especially when Hunter's face looked so relaxed and peaceful.

Tomorrow they *would* rescue their loved ones from those monsters, and a large part of their souls could finally begin to heal. It was only the comfort of that thought that allowed Kylie to finally relax her mind and worries enough to drift off as well.

CHAPTER TWENTY-FOUR

*F*or the umpteenth time, Kylie picked at the very uncomfortable swat-like black vest she was wearing as Hunter, Maxim, and she drove in an Explorer they borrowed from Lev's brother up the highway to Amarillo. The sun was barely peeking over the eastern horizon, but Kylie wasn't in the least bit sleepy.

Dressed from head-to-toe in black, every piece of her outfit had been duplicated from the clothes the lioness assassin had been wearing when she had attacked them at Karen's house. Hunter had told her about it beforehand, and she had agreed that it was the best way to be seen when they drove up to the gates of the ranch, but now that she was actually wearing it, along with the blonde wig that had been her own idea, she felt as though she was cosplaying rather than acting as a true decoy.

Her companions were dressed casually in jeans, sweatshirts, and hiking boots, though Kylie knew that both carried a concealed Glock holstered to their sides. Kylie prayed that neither man would have to use them. It was no small comfort that both were just as lethal in their shifted forms.

She and Hunter sat in the back while Maxim drove, and Kylie was immensely grateful for the comforting hand Hunter had threaded in her own. It was the anchor she needed to keep her fear and nervousness at bay for the important part she was about to play. Hunter was staring down at his cell phone, reading a text that had just come in from one of Maxim's wolves.

"The geneticist is still at home," Hunter announced. "We may have to storm the house and abduct him if he doesn't plan on going to the ranch today."

"We'll give it another couple of hours," Maxim replied. "That'll give all the various groups more than enough time to get into position."

Kylie's stomach lurched with renewed nerves. She was *really* beginning to regret eating breakfast.

Hunter squeezed her hand, and she turned to him questionably. "It's not too late for you to back out," he said. "You know that I'd rather you had stayed back at Lev's place with Sasha, anyway. Maxim and I could easily create another kind of distraction."

Kylie scowled. "You can stop right there. Me going in as a lioness is the best way to make sure both you and Maxim get into the ranch without having to run through a rain of bullets."

"If the bobcats do their part well, then all of us may be able to get inside without being shot at even once," Hunter argued.

"Yeah, *if*," Kylie said dryly. "I'm not willing to make that bet with either of your lives just because I'm a little nervous."

Maxim snorted. "A little? I can smell your fear all the way up here."

"Even so, I'm still doing this," Kylie retorted stubbornly.

Hunter sighed. "It was worth another shot."

"We're almost to Amarillo," Maxim announced. "We'll park and wait for the others to pick us up with the doc's car at the Westgate Mall as planned."

Kylie sighed. The next two hours would no doubt be the longest in her life.

***

"They're here," Maxim said abruptly, making Kylie

jump.

She had been staring out the window at the sea of cars surrounding them, thinking about Molly and her mother and what she was going to say to them when she finally saw them. And she *would* see her mother today. She refused to believe otherwise.

A silver Audi slowly drove by before parking in a slot at the end of the lane.

Hunter opened his door and released her hand. "This is it."

Kylie swallowed hard against the huge knot that had suddenly formed in her throat and nodded sharply at him. Time to implement the next stage of her disguise.

She took her mother's charm bracelet off and snapped open the small charm with the stylized "L" engraved into the silver on each side. She quickly rubbed the pad of her index finger along the inside walls of both halves just to be sure before closing the charm and stuffing the bracelet deep into her pants pocket.

Once the smell of lion reached her nose, she pulled the thick, leather hood attached to her vest over her head until half her face was concealed, the edges of the material touching the tip of her nose. Then with a deep breath to steady herself, she climbed out of the vehicle where Hunter was already waiting for her. She saw his nose flare once, but he said nothing as they followed Maxim down to the silver car.

Maxim exchanged keys with the driver of the Audi, a wolf Kylie didn't recognize, but it was the man in the backseat with a split lip and a swollen, darkening eye trying to glare a hole through the window and into the side of Maxim's head that had her complete attention. She felt a wash of hatred flow through her at the blatant look of outrage on the bastard's face. She couldn't fathom the type of evil a person would have to have inside to experiment on and torture another living creature without batting an eye and then feel outraged that someone had dared taken offense to his work and would attack him like this. At least his mouth was duct taped shut so they wouldn't be forced to listen to his vileness the whole way to the ranch.

It was in that moment that Kylie's fear and nervousness disappeared completely. It was the first time she was glad that she had been born a Polyshifter, that because of her unique ability to shift into a lion, she could contribute to the operation that would bring down the lions' ranch and all its horrors, but more importantly, all their loved ones would be saved.

"Be careful back there with that piece of trash," Kylie told Hunter as she moved to circle around the front of the car as far away from the three wolves that had exited it as possible.

They had all been told that Kylie would be wearing the scent of a lioness curtesy of the assassin they had taken prisoner as part of their deception, but she didn't want to get too close and allow them to get a good whiff of her and realize that the scent of lion was too strong and fresh to just be coming from her clothing.

"Follow us until you get a quarter of a mile away and then hide the SUV at the designated spot," Maxim instructed. "We'll be counting on you three to run interference should any of us have a tail once we've rescued all the captives."

Kylie waited until the three were nearly to Lev's brother's SUV before walking over to the front passenger door and slipping into the front seat. Hunter was already seated next to the geneticist and was sticking a piece of tape lightly over his mouth. Kylie winced internally, hoping he wouldn't have to rip it off or he would be losing a good portion of his facial hair.

Through the rearview mirror, Kylie saw their lion captive's eyes widen in utter shock, then narrow in rage, the word "traitor" practically radiated from them. Muffled screams that were probably expletives broke the silence, but none of them paid the geneticist any mind. He finally subsided once they were back on the highway heading west out of the city.

Kylie kept her eyes looking straight ahead and her

body alert, doing her best to mimic what she remembered of the body language of the lioness assassin. No
one said a word the entire ride to the ranch, the silence
only broken when the geneticist abruptly gasped. Her
eyes flickered to the rearview mirror again in enough
time to see him slump over, his seatbelt the only thing
preventing him from falling over completely.

Hunter pushed him back until his back and bound
hands rested against the seat and positioned the lolling
head to rest against the man's own shoulder. He then
tucked the empty syringe in his hand into the pocket
of the seat in front of him and settled into a similar
position, playing the part of a captured and unconscious co-conspirator.

"It's show time," Maxim muttered. He turned the
car onto a single-lane dirt road that cut through a mini-
forest of mesquite trees.

Kylie suddenly felt the uncanny sensation of doz-
ens of eyes on her, and she had to fight down a growl,
not sure if they were indeed being watched or if it was
just her imagination because she knew their allies were
out there somewhere.

About a half-mile down, a metal gate came into
view that stretched across the road, the gate, according
to Jack, connected to an electrified fence that spanned
the entire perimeter of the property. A small, white
building sat on the side of the road outside the fence

about a meter or two out. A guard station.

Maxim pulled up to it without any hesitation and rolled down his window. Some of the bobcat sharpshooters had been tasked with taking care of the guards that had been posted all along the entrance road before they could alert the guard station of the Audi's approach, and given that no one had shot at them yet, they had been successful.

However, the real test was now.

Kylie turned her head towards Maxim's window just as the guard barked, "Who the hell are you?"

She knew the exact moment the man saw her because he suddenly went utterly still and his heart literally stuttered in fear. It was said that even members of the lion clans feared their assassins, that they lived in constant fear of pissing off someone in a higher echelon and finding one of the Alpha's assassins on their doorstep.

"It appears we have a little problem," Kylie said casually, staring intensely at the lion shifter even though her hood kept him from seeing her eyes.

"I-I—" the security guard stammered, his demeanor screaming how desperately he wanted to flee.

"Imagine my surprise when our Alpha pulled me from another job in order to clean up your colossal fuck-up a few days ago. Then I come here and find that it wasn't so much as a fuck-up but likely a deliberate act of treason." She gestured with her head towards the backseat, and the lion finally noticed the geneticist and Hunter.

Kylie didn't think his face could become any paler. "I—I see."

"A word of warning," Kylie continued, proud that her voice remained strong and deadly. "Although I have thus far found you and this station's other workers innocent of this man's treachery, that will change if you alert those in the compound that I am coming."

CHAPTER TWENTY-FIVE

$\mathcal{K}$ ylie didn't release the breath she was holding until their car had rounded the house and parked right next to a wide, steel door between the attached garage and the house she had seen in the photo with Molly without a single shot being fired at the car.

"Keep sharp," Maxim muttered out of the corner of his mouth. "There's a couple of armed lions heading our way, so we'll unfortunately have to go with plan B."

Hunter cursed. That meant Kylie's little act was over, and she would now have to accompany them down into the bowels of the ranch.

"As soon as they reach the car," Maxim continued, "the bobcats'll tranq them. Once that happens, the gig will be up, and we'll only have a few seconds to reach the door and get inside before any guards within eyesight will likely start shooting. Let's just hope my guys were able to disable all the electric locks or this'll get real ugly fast."

Although Hunter remained slumped against the seat, and kept his eyes closed, he had already removed the tape across his mouth, and one hand was beneath his sweatshirt, no doubt curled around his gun.

The next few minutes happened in a blur.

Kylie remembered seeing the two approaching men drop almost in slow motion before she was scrabbling out of the car, nearly bumping into Hunter as he moved past his opened car door. Hunter reflexively grabbed Kylie's arm as the two of them made a beeline for the metal door. Gunfire sounded loudly behind them, close enough that it could have been Maxim firing, but then a bullet hit the bricks near Hunter's right shoulder just as she reached out for the doorknob.

She nearly sobbed when it turned easily, and she was able to pull it open. Hunter shoved her inside so hard that she stumbled and nearly fell to her knees. Hunter grabbed her arm again to steady her as the door slammed behind them.

"Come on!" Maxim exclaimed, gesturing towards a lone door at the far end of what turned out to be a completely empty room no larger than a wide corridor. "I can't lock the door, and there's at least a dozen of them only minutes behind us. I'm not sure even the bobcats can pick them all off before one or two can get inside. I'm afraid we don't have time to wait for the rescue group coming through the front to meet up with us here like we planned. That door at the end should open to the emergency stairwell Jack mentioned."

Hunter pulled Kylie tightly against him and threaded their hands together tightly. "Don't leave my side unless you absolutely have to! Maxim, we've got your rear."

"Maybe I should go first," Kylie said as they raced to the stairwell. "They might freeze just like that guard when they smell—"

"Absolutely not!" both men snarled in unison.

"As soon as we get in the stairwell, you need to change back into a jaguar," Hunter said in a tone that brooked no argument. "Soon our guys will be down below helping us look for captives and mining information. If we get separated, there's a good chance they might attack you without realizing who you are if they smell lion."

Once through the door and they were descending a narrow set of industrial, metal steps, Kylie dug out her bracelet and began fumbling with the charms in the poor lighting.

"We'll go down three levels first," Maxim said.

"That's the only place we know for sure other than the lowest level labs that they were holding the captives. Hopefully they won't have moved your brother somewhere else as a precaution after Jack's escape. Then we'll search the other floors one by one, room by fucking room, until we find everyone. With the locks in the whole building disengaged, some of them may even be trying to escape on their own."

Kylie completely expected to hear the sound of the door crashing open above, bracing herself for the exchange of bullets that were sure to follow, but before she knew it, the door to the third basement level was before them without a single shot being fired just as she finally managed to find the right charm and pop it open. Then she nearly dropped the bracelet with her finger still pressed against the hollow inside one of the halves when a crash sounded above them and Hunter yanked her hard through the door.

A young man in a lab coat stood frozen in the brightly illuminated hallway lined with closed doors they found themselves in, his chest heaving, and staring at them as if they were some type of hideous monsters birthed by the stairwell. Maxim was on him before Kylie could even gasp in alarm, punching him square in the face. The guy's head snapped back with a cringe-inducing crack, and he instantly crumbled to the ground.

"You two take the doors on the right," Maxim said and immediately hurried over to the first one on the left.

The first room was completely empty except for a couple of suspicious dark stains along one of the walls. The second appeared to be jammed. Hunter kicked it open, but this one, too, was empty. The fact that they were empty really didn't surprise her. If these rooms were where they locked up their captives when they weren't being tortured, then she didn't think those types of monsters would bother to provide their victims with a blanket, much less a bed.

Then Maxim let out a startled noise, and Hunter and she were immediately at his back where he was looking into a darkened room with an expression of pure horror. Kylie nearly gagged at the smell coming out of that room, an unholy mixture of animal waste, death, and something she had never smelled before. Certain she didn't want to see what lay within that darkness, Kylie forced herself to look anyway. Even in the darkness, she knew that the blob that was a lighter shade of darkness curled against the far wall was the body of an animal.

Kylie hastily got out of the way as Maxim back-pedalled and shut the door. "That was probably the coyote shifter Jack mentioned," he said, so angry that his words were barely more than a series of growls.

"We can't help him anymore."

She grabbed onto Hunter's arm, feeling both sick and furious. How awful it must have been, to have died all alone in the cold darkness after you had lost your mind to the point of completely losing your humanity, terrified and in unimaginable pain. That all of their missing loved ones must have been forced to live locked up like this for months, for years...

A snarl fell from her lips. She wanted to go back to the young man in the lab coat Maxim had decked and rip out his throat with her teeth, to go back above and do the same to the piece of shit geneticist they'd left in the car. But then Hunter said one word that instantly snapped her out of the killing rage she had inadvertently fallen into.

"Ryder."

Kylie shook her head violently. What was wrong with her? She had to get it together, dammit! There were people counting on her right now.

Without a word, Kylie followed Hunter to the next door and then to the next, moving down corridor after corridor until they had all been opened and searched and they found themselves at a different stairwell than the one they had left with no sign of another living soul.

"Up or down?" Maxim asked.

"Down," Hunter said immediately. "The others

are probably searching the two floors above us as we speak. While this floor reeks of various shifters, none of the scents are particularly fresh. Either they were moved because of Jack's escape, or we tripped a silent alarm that your people didn't catch and they were fore-warned to move them somewhere deeper and likely more protected."

"Then maybe we should wait for the others to catch up," Kylie said. "We could very well step into a room full of lions with guns rather than needles."

She fully expected Hunter to at least argue with her—she could practically taste the urgency to find his brother rolling off him—so she was shocked when both men nodded.

"Let's return to the other stairwell," Maxim suggested. "Once we meet up, half can follow me down this one while the other half continue down the other with you two."

Retracing their steps, they had nearly reached the door to the stairwell when a hail of gunfire erupted from somewhere above, freezing them where they stood for a few, heart-pounding seconds. Unfortunately, the door didn't have a window as some stairwell entrances did.

"Get into that room!" Hunter hissed, steering Kylie by the elbow towards the first room they had inspected, his Glock clutched tightly in his right hand.

Then the stairwell door exploded open before she could move more than a couple of steps, and a mass of bodies spilled into the hall.

CHAPTER TWENTY-SIX

"Shit!" Hunter snarled, bringing his gun around to face these newest invaders—only to let out a surprised laugh. "You guys fucking scared the shit out of us!" he hissed.

Kylie turned around and saw several familiar faces. Her shoulders sagged in relief.

"We'd hoped you all had gotten down this far when we didn't run into you topside," one of the tigers whose name her frazzled brain couldn't remember at the moment said.

"How many are shooting at you?" Maxim demanded.

"At least a dozen. They came from somewhere within the house, itself, I think. As far as we could tell, the bobcats took out all the security guards outside before we even made it in."

"I guess we'll all have to use the other stairs," Maxim said. "Follow us. We were just waiting for you all before heading down to continue the search."

"Have you been able to locate any of the captives?" Hunter asked as they hurried down the corridor.

"Just one," one of the wolves answered, and Kylie's pulse suddenly sped up. "She looked pretty bad, practically skin and bones, but we're pretty sure it was Jack's mate, Maya. A couple of my clansmen are trying to get her out as we speak."

Even though it hadn't been Molly or her mother, Kylie felt a surge of happiness and was suddenly more hopeful. Finding the dead coyote shifter had shaken her confidence. If one of them had been found still alive, then there was still a better than average chance all the others would be found alive, too.

"We found the coyote," Hunter said grimly. "He was already dead. It was terrible, what that poor man must have gone through to end in such an unspeakable state."

Once they reached the door, a couple of the tigers pushed to the front and peered into the dim stairwell before they allowed everyone to enter. Seconds later they were at the door to the fourth basement level and the tigers repeated the process.

"Another hallway full of doors," one reported. "Some of them are open, and I can see a desk covered with papers in one. Should we stop?"

"Yes," Maxim said instantly. "A couple of you stay on this level and see if you can find any useful intel on what these bastards are doing here."

The next level had something large and heavy barricading the door. It took five men to push the door open wide enough for everyone to squeeze through. The first thing Kylie noticed was the sound of pounding footsteps somewhere nearby, followed by the enormous room on the left that had a large viewing window that reminded her of an ICU room. However, the equipment inside made the space look like a cross between a morgue, a torture dungeon, and a server farm.

Two large metal slabs about the length of a tall man sat side-by-side in the center of a room that was lined with at least a couple dozen computers, a series of attached thick, leather and metal restraints dangling off both edges. There was also a wide cart of stainless steel drawers covered on top with every type of medical tool imaginable as well as some wicked looking items that Kylie had no idea what they could possibly be used for except to cause pain.

Maxim suddenly went rigid, and his nostril flared.

"I can smell Anna in here," he whispered, his tone equal parts horror and hope. Kylie immediately sniffed the air, and sure enough, there was a strong odor of several male lions and a fainter smell of tiger beneath. Her heart clenched when she also caught the acrid smell of fear and blood. What the hell were these bastards *doing*?

"Come on," Hunter said firmly, placing a hand on Maxim's shoulder. "Her scent is still strong enough that she might still be on this floor. It also looks like whoever was here left in a big hurry. All the computers are still on and some of the carts are skewed."

Maxim nodded, the haunted look in his eyes replaced with a cold fury. Sandwiched between the newly arrived men, they moved quickly down the hall, checking every door until they came to one that was locked and couldn't be kicked in after several tries. There was no doorknob, and on closer inspection, seemed to be dead-bolted from the inside with a non-electronic lock.

"I bet a bunch of the sick fuckers are hiding inside," one of the tigers growled as he gave the door another savage kick. "It's lined with something—concrete or steel. There's no way we're getting in this way."

"Oh, we're getting in," Maxim said, his voice quiet and utterly lethal. Kylie actually felt a shiver go down her spine. "And then we'll make them *talk*."

He stalked over to an adjacent room, and everyone silently followed him inside. Then without a word, he began kicking in the sheetrock of the wall connecting the two rooms. All the rest instantly joined him.

Not knowing how much help she could be, Kylie stood back out of everyone's way, anxiously watching the door and listening for footsteps. She hadn't forgotten the fading footsteps she had heard when they had first entered this level. The last thing they needed was to be ambushed here, especially when Maxim was in so much emotional pain and not at his sharpest.

A gunshot abruptly sounded and several guys cursed. Kylie whipped around, her heart suddenly in her throat. "Everyone okay?" she asked anxiously.

Nods all around.

"That definitely came from the other side," Hunter said, peering briefly into the center of the large hole they had managed to tear in the wall before stepping back and to the side. He stared thoughtfully at the hole. "I have an idea."

He edged closer to the hole and crouched down. "We're trying to save you, you idiot!" he shouted. "The place is overrun with enemy shifters, communications are down, and we don't have much time! How about you unbolt the damn door before they torch the place and you end up burning alive in there?"

Kylie stared at her lover in astonishment for a split-second before she scrambled out of the room and back to the bolted door, everyone else a half-step behind her. Then they heard several clicks in succession, and the door was opening. Maxim lunged forward and the person at the door was brutally pushed back as he charged inside, Hunter and a couple of tigers right on Maxim's heels.

"Stay back!" she heard an unknown baritone voice say shrilly, dripping with panic and fear. "I'll kill them!"

Kylie's eyes widened, and she pushed into the room even though a couple of wolves tried to keep her out. She froze the moment the scene was finally revealed.

"Molly…" she tried to say, but her friend's name got caught in the huge knot of horror that had instantly formed in her throat.

A middle-aged man in a lab coat that was drenched in blood all down the front stood next to two women on the floor, one of which was Molly who was hugging, Kylie suddenly realized with more horror, Maxim's fiancé, Anna, to her chest. Molly's hands and the front of the white hospital gown she wore were stained with crimson, as was the bottom half of Anna's gown that was wadded between her legs. There was also a pool of blood that was slowly spreading out from beneath Anna's bottom.

To add to the horror show, the bastard lion was pointing a gun at the back of Molly's head while she held Anna and attempted to shield the bleeding woman's body with her own. Molly's eyes were closed tightly, and she appeared to be mumbling something under her breath, maybe a prayer. If not for the faint rising of her chest, Kylie would have thought Anna dead.

Molly cried out in pain and her eyes snapped open as the lion suddenly reached out and grabbed a handful of her hair, yanking her head back. It was in that eternal moment that Molly's eyes found Kylie's, and their gazes locked. Kylie would never forget the look of shock when Molly finally saw beyond the disguise, of the anguish and absolute terror in her best friend's eyes for the rest of her life.

"You're going to stand aside and allow me to walk out of here with this human," the scientist snarled, "or I'll put a bullet in both of them right now before you can even pull—"

Kylie wasn't sure how it happened. One moment she blinked and the next, Maxim was suddenly *there* in his tiger form, his powerful jaws biting down on the lion's neck with a disturbing *crunch* until he had bitten clean through the lion's neck. His severed head fell out of a sudden fountain of blood with a gruesome, meaty *thump* onto the floor next to Molly. The gun went off as both body and tiger hit the ground, and Molly finally screamed. However, the bullet wedged harmlessly into the ceiling.

Her legs were moving towards the two women on the floor before Kylie had even made a conscious decision to do so. She dropped down to her knees beside Anna and began to stuff more of the bleeding woman's hospital gown hard against her groin. She wanted nothing more than to throw her arms around Molly in relief that her best friend was okay, to reassure her, but right now nothing else mattered more than to try and staunch the blood, not even the fact that she was now touching tiger's blood and her dominant shifter soul was likely now a tiger as well.

Then Molly was talking, and it took Kylie a bewildered moment for her friend's words to compute, and that Molly was actually making sense and not screeching hysterically.

"That fucker said she'd had a miscarriage. She was already bleeding pretty badly when he dragged her in here and just dumped her in a corner. While he was babbling into his cell phone, I tried to stop the bleeding, but nothing I did seemed to work at all!"

"We need to get her to a hospital *now*!" A naked Maxim knelt down on Anna's other side and reached beneath her to lift her up into his arms. Kylie stood with him, her hands maintaining the pressure against the flow of blood.

"Go with them, Kylie," Hunter said. "Help Maxim get both Anna and Molly out of this hellhole. Ryder's still waiting for me, and your mother—I swear if she's here, I'll bring her to you. Now go!"

Feeling torn, Kylie could only nod in anguish. The thought of leaving Hunter behind—but no, he was right. Maxim and Molly were counting on her, and it was her fault in the first place that Molly was even here in the middle of all this madness and horror.

"Find them. Then come back to me."

CHAPTER TWENTY-SEVEN

There was a sole shifter clinic on the eastern edge of Amarillo, but even as they raced across the city at probably over a hundred miles an hour where the tiger that was driving them was able, Kylie knew it was no use. Anna wasn't just bleeding from a miscarriage, she was bleeding from whatever experiment those bastards had been performing on her. Without knowing exactly what had been done, there was no way the shifter doctors could quickly know how to treat her.

Her eyes had fluttered open once, but Kylie doubted the poor girl was truly seeing anything or even aware of her situation. Maxim had tried to talk to her, but she hadn't responded to any of his words. She had to bite her lip hard to keep from bursting into tears at the pain Maxim was radiating, how he gently cradled her head in his lap and kissed her forehead tenderly as he trembled and willed with all his being for her to hold on.

They had managed to reach the surface in a surprisingly short amount of time, and the bobcats had indeed cleared the property of any security. Still, Kylie couldn't help tormenting herself with the fruitless wish that they had gotten to Anna and Molly sooner.

Molly was sitting quietly in the third row of the Explorer. Kylie had expected her to fall apart the moment they were in the SUV and she realized they were finally safe. Yet, Molly hadn't even shed one tear, much less gone into hysterics. Kylie was certain her friend had seen Maxim shift into a tiger, bite the head off that piece of scum, and then shift back into a man, but she didn't even seem to be nervous about being in a vehicle with him at all. Was she in shock?

However, they were pulling into the parking lot of what looked on first glance like an apartment complex, and she lost the moment to start fussing over her friend. They had called ahead, so there was already a crowd of people waiting for them at the entrance. Once Anna was removed from the SUV, Kylie hung back for a moment, asking the driver to wait a moment before going to park.

Even though Kylie had probably let the cat out of the bag about her Polyshifter heritage in front of all those tigers and wolves, it was still possible that in all the excitement, none of the men had even noticed the change in her scent. So just in case her situation could still be salvaged, she needed to make her jaguar soul dominant again.

She took off the swat-like vest and then used a towel she had found in the pocket of one of the seats and a water bottle to rinse and wipe her skin clean of Anna's blood, paying special attention to beneath her nails. Only then did she use the charm bracelet.

Molly watched all of this without comment, even reaching a hand out for the towel after Kylie had finished with it where she proceeded to clean the blood from her hand as well. Her continued silence was making Kylie more and more worried.

"Come on," Kylie said, opening her door, "Let's get you checked out inside, too."

Molly shook her head as she climbed over the seat and followed Kylie out her door. "I'm okay."

"Like hell you are!" Kylie finally exploded, whirling around to face the other girl. "You were just kidnapped by a bunch of psychos who did God-only-knows what to you, only to watch a girl nearly bleed to death right in front of you while her boyfriend turns into a tiger right before your eyes and literally bites his head off!"

"So the tiger part was real," Molly said softly. "I

thought maybe I had hallucinated that part, that they'd drugged my food or something, and I was just tripping out. Everything did taste kinda funny…"

Kylie instantly deflated as her worry was replaced by a heavy dose of guilt. She threw her arms around the redhead and hugged her tight. "I'm so sorry. This whole mess is my fault, because of what I am, because those bastards wanted to draw me out."

"'What you are'?" Molly repeated, pulling out of her embrace to look at Kylie with a perplexed frown.

"I promise to tell you everything," Kylie said, tugging on Molly's arm, "but first, I want you to get checked out by a doctor. Those sick bastards really might have put something in your food."

Once Molly had submitted to some blood tests and promised to find the doctor again if she started to feel ill, the clinic staff had given her a pair of scrubs to wear and allowed her to go on her way without admitting her, at least until her labs came back and required otherwise. They had immediately sought out Maxim in the clinic's version of an ER where they found out that Anna had been rushed into surgery. A nurse led them to a waiting room where they had directed Maxim.

As he had arrived naked, he too had been given a pair of scrubs. He was a mess. Kylie sat next to him and wrapped her arms around him, offering him what

little comfort she could. Maxim wasn't physically crying, but the utter despair in his eyes told her that his
soul was wailing in anguish.

After a long silence, Kylie began to quietly tell
Molly about herself, about shifters and their society in
general, and then what it meant to be what she was, a
Polyshifter who had once been a Deadend and was
now considered a Returner of the jaguar clan. She explained about being attacked by the lioness and why
the assassin had thought she was a Rogue from a lion
clan.

Then finally, she told her about her relationship
with Hunter and why he had stayed behind at the
ranch.

"So you *do* know who your birth parents are,"
Molly said.

Her eyes were looking a little glazed. Understandable, as it wasn't every day that you learned there were
people in the world who could shapeshift into animals
at will and that one was your best friend since elementary school.

Kylie nodded. "Their names are Alan and Grace
Hall. They were both Polyshifters, too."

"And you think your mother was in that horrible
place?" Molly said, appalled.

"Another captive who managed to escape said he

saw a woman who looked just like me and was a cougar shifter. Just as I'm now living as a jaguar, my mom and dad lived as cougars in order to hide their true selves, so it's possible."

Maxim lifted his head. "If she's there, Hunter will find her," he said firmly.

Kylie smiled sadly and hugged him tighter. Even though he was in agony, he was still trying to cheer her up. The man's strength and selflessness was boggling.

Anna was still in surgery when there was a big commotion outside the waiting room. Kylie rose and peeked out the door in enough time to see a group of doctors and nurses wheeling a stretcher quickly down the hall that contained a bleeding, dark-haired man dressed only in a pair of blood-spattered scrub pants that was wearing an oxygen mask. She stiffened when she caught the whiff of a jaguar.

"Kylie!"

Her head immediately whipped towards the voice. Hunter was currently hurrying down the hall towards them, the front of his sweatshirt covered in blood. Just how many times was she going to see her loved ones smeared in blood today?

She ran to meet him, throwing her arms around him and squeezing him tight despite the blood. It smelled of jaguar, so she was in no danger of switching animal souls.

"Was that...?" she asked anxiously, suddenly re-alizing who the man on the stretcher must have been.

"Yes, that was Ryder," Hunter replied, his voice just as anxious. "We found him wandering around the sixth level. One of the bastards had shot him in the abdomen before he managed to take him down."

"And my mother?" She was almost afraid to hear the answer.

Hunter looked stricken, and Kylie's heart felt as if it had suddenly been cut out. "Is she—" Her voice cracked. "Is she—dead?"

"I don't know," he said. "We looked everywhere. By the time we found Ryder, we'd already found all the other women Jack had mentioned minus a cougar. Even so, some of the guys stayed behind in order to give the place another sweep. We think most of the scientists managed to escape in the very beginning, through that second stairwell. All their vehicles are missing from the garage, including the Audi with the geneticist. It's very possible that they could have taken her with them then. She *is* a Polyshifter, after all, but we have no way of knowing right now if she was even there in the first place. The guys are also gathering every file, paper, and computer they can get their hands on. Whatever they were doing there, hopefully we'll find the answers in all of that."

His eyes suddenly looked over her shoulder, and

Kylie automatically turned to look as well. Molly was currently looking out the door, staring curiously at them.

"Molly's okay, and Anna's still in surgery," she said. Then in a lower voice, "It doesn't look good, and Maxim knows it. That she even survived the ride over here is a miracle."

Kylie introduced Molly and Hunter, then her lover went over to Maxim and put a comforting arm around his shoulder. They began talking in low voices.

"Come on," Kylie said to her friend, dragging her back into the hall. "Let's give them a little privacy for the moment and go see if we can find a vending machine in this place. It's going to be a long day."

CHAPTER TWENTY-EIGHT

*I*t was a little before noon when Sasha arrived, and the moment the siblings hugged, she thought Maxim would finally break down and cry. When he didn't, Kylie was more than a little worried. She was afraid that if the worst did indeed happen, then he would shatter with all that pent up emotion.

Anna was still in surgery a couple of hours later when a doctor came to inform Hunter that Ryder's surgery had gone well and they had just moved him into a recovery room. Kylie was immensely glad that Sasha was there to support and comfort Maxim as Hunter needed to be with Ryder now and she needed to be there for Hunter.

Ryder was still under the anesthesia when they entered his room. He was now breathing on his own with only the help of a little extra oxygen through a nose catheter. As Hunter pulled over a chair and sat down next to his brother's bed, Kylie opted to stand next to him for the time being while Molly took the only other chair next to the door.

For a long while, she studied Ryder's face. The shape seemed a bit wider than Hunter's, but she wasn't sure if it was because his face was a little swollen and distorted from the multiple bruising throughout. They had the same black hair, and she knew from the picture Maxim had passed around that Ryder also had hazel eyes.

"You two look so much alike," Kylie said softly as she ran her fingers through Hunter's hair soothingly.

Hunter nodded. "Even after not seeing him for over a year, I'm surprised at how much he still looks the same. A little thinner, yes, but no shock there."

Speaking of shock... "I'm worried about Maxim," Kylie said hesitantly.

Again, he nodded. "I am, too. I've never seen him keep his emotions to himself to this extent. I was actually glad to see him release his rage on that lion. We've both been holding it all in ever since Jack told us about Ryder and Anna, but unlike me, he didn't have someone to distract him from the worst of it. He was a ticking time bomb as you glimpsed yesterday.

This though—the way he is now—this is a million times worse."

Kylie bent down and hugged him around the neck. "All we can do is stay by his side as much as we can."

"You guys are already so close," Molly suddenly cut in. She mock-frowned at Kylie. "I can't believe you didn't tell me about him. We should all wish that our fathers had 'friends' like him." The last was said sarcastically.

Kylie winced, remembering the lie she had fed Molly the night the redhead had brought her the bracelet.

"Very few humans know about us," Hunter said. "She would've been in a lot of trouble if she had told you and you flipped out about it and went running to the nearest TV station to scream it to the world."

"She's not going to get in trouble now, is she?" Molly fretted.

He shook his head. "No, because it was the lions' own damned fault for dragging you into our world. As long as you don't do any interviews, everything'll be fine."

"Speaking of," Kylie said. "We need to start thinking about what we're going to tell Tara—oh my God!" Her eyes widened in dismay. "I can't believe I *forgot*! We think Ty went missing the same night as you!

The cops found human blood in your apartment!"

For a split-second, Molly looked alarmed, but then she shook her head. "Actually, we had a big fight earlier that day and broke up. He probably went down to Houston for the weekend to sulk at his brother's house. I wouldn't be surprised if he turned his phone off in case I called. He would've probably ignored any of Tara's or your calls, too."

Kylie sagged in relief against Hunter's back. "Thank God."

"The blood," Molly continued, "it was probably mine. I ended up with a bloody nose trying to fight the bastard who took me. He was wearing a black ski mask like some cheesy burglar, if you can believe it."

"The sound of a woman's voice that isn't scream-ing," a deep, unfamiliar voice abruptly rasped, making all of them instantly turn their eyes to the bed, "that's something I never thought I would hear again."

Hunter made a sound deep in his throat that sounded suspiciously as though he was choking back a sob. "Welcome back, bro."

"Seeing you here—" Ryder's expression became pinched, as if he was trying not to cry, "I was afraid seeing you come for me down in that pit of hell was something I had dreamed while delirious. It's hap-pened before." He closed his eyes, and this time, a sin-gle tear did fall from the corner of his right eye.

Kylie felt her throat tighten with the threat of tears, herself.

Hunter reached over and clasped Ryder's hand tightly. "Of course I came. I'm here, and you're going to be okay."

Ryder smiled and then slowly wiped his eyes with the side of his free hand, careful not to jostle the IV inserted into the back of it.

"So, are you going to tell me who these lovely ladies are?"

Hunter grinned. "Ryder, meet Kylie Moore." He paused and then turned to look heatedly at Kylie. "…my mate-to-be if she'll have me."

The incredulous look in Ryder's eyes was priceless.

In that moment as her mind whirled in something like shock, Kylie found herself wishing with all her soul that another miracle would happen, that she would be wrong, and Maxim would get his happy ending as well. Anna had survived this long into the surgery. Surely that had to be a good sign? Because she didn't ever want to see that man break.

Kylie looked from Ryder to Hunter and felt her lips curve up into an answering smile that was bittersweet.

There was still one thing missing from this moment. How close had she come to actually finding her mother today? Hopefully the data they had taken from the lions' ranch would offer her an answer. Maybe it would even have an answer to the whereabouts of her father.

Once they returned to Riverford, she also hoped for a chance to talk to Karen face-to-face in order to find out the truth of that security footage. Even if it turned out that Karen had been lying to them from the beginning, Kylie still wanted to know, though deep down she didn't really believe that would turn out to be the truth.

"I'll be a handful," she warned seriously, giving Hunter one last chance to take back his proposal. "We may even need to spend a lot of time in Great Britain if you catch my meaning."

He laughed. Now that he had his brother back safe, if not yet completely sound, Hunter's eyes seemed to blaze with life. "I'm counting on it. What's life without a little intrigue?"

ABOUT THE AUTHOR

Cristina Rayne is a *New York Times* and *USA Today* bestselling author who lives in West Texas with her crazy cat and about a dozen bookcases full of fantasy worlds and steamy romances. She has a degree in Computer Science which totally qualifies her to write romances. As Fantasy is her first love, she feels if she can inject a little love into the fantastical, along with a few steamy scenes, then all the better. She is also the author of the *Claimed by the Elven King* and *Erotic Tales from the Vampire Underground* series.

www.CristinaRayneAuthor.com

RESCUED? BY THE WOLF: A SHORT STORY

After dealing with the aftermath of her uncontrollable heat and finding a severely wounded wolf shifter within Hunter's forest territory, Kylie is put in a dangerous position where she must choose between saving two lives and revealing her secret to the worst possible person.

TEMPTED BY THE TIGER
BOOK THREE
Coming Fall 2015

It's been a year since the rescue operation launched against the lions' compound of horrors, and not only is Kylie no closer to finding out the fate of her parents, but she soon learns that the lions have found the location of her mother's clan and plan to attack, pushing Hunter and her to leave for Great Britain to search for the clan's location in order to warn them. However, after two weeks pass without so much as a text from the couple, Maxim Clarke follows in their wake where it soon becomes apparent that he isn't the only one interested in finding his missing friends, nor is he as recovered from the tragedy of what happened to Anna as he had thought.

Made in the USA
San Bernardino, CA
22 November 2015